Dear Reader,

Welcome to the town of Hard Luck, Alaska! I hope you'll join me there to meet the Midnight Sons, their families, friends and wives-to-be.

The people I want to credit with the idea for this project are, in fact, fictional—they're Valerie, Stephanie and Norah, the three sisters I wrote about in the Orchard Valley trilogy (Harlequin Romances #3232, 3239, 3244). I loved writing those books, I loved the characters and the town and last but definitely not least, I loved the way readers responded to the stories.

So when Harlequin suggested this six-book project, I was thrilled. Soon after that, the town of Hard Luck, the O'Halloran brothers and Midnight Sons all came to life. Never have I worked harder on a project, nor have I enjoyed my research more. In the summer of 1994, my husband and I traveled to Alaska, and I fell in love with the state—its sheer magnificence, the warmth of its people, the excitement of life on the "last frontier."

Now I invite you to sit back, put your feet up and allow me to introduce you to some proud, stubborn, *wonderful* men—Alaskan men—and show you what happens when they meet their real matches. Women from the "lower forty-eight." Women with the courage to change their lives and take risks for love. Women a lot like you and me!

Love,

Debbie

Debbie Macomber is one of the most popular romance authors writing today. She's written more than seventy romances (for Harlequin and Silhouette) and several bestselling "mainstream" women's fiction novels. Not surprisingly, Debbie has won a number of awards for her books.

She lives in Washington State with her husband, Wayne, and their dog, Peterkins. They have four grown children—and they've just become grandparents! Debbie's *thrilled* with her new granddaughter, Jazmine Lynn.

Debbie loves to hear from her readers. You can reach her at: P.O. Box 1458, Port Orchard, Washington 98366.

Books by Debbie Macomber

HARLEQUIN ROMANCE

Don't miss any of our special offers. Write to us at the following address for information on our newest releases.

Harlequin Reader Service
U.S.: 3010 Walden Ave., P.O. Box 1325, Buffalo, NY 14269
Canadian: P.O. Box 609, Fort Erie, Ont. L2A 5X3

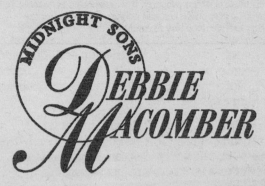

MIDNIGHT SONS

DEBBIE MACOMBER

The Marriage Risk

Harlequin Books

TORONTO • NEW YORK • LONDON
AMSTERDAM • PARIS • SYDNEY • HAMBURG
STOCKHOLM • ATHENS • TOKYO • MILAN
MADRID • WARSAW • BUDAPEST • AUCKLAND

ISBN 0-373-03383-4

THE MARRIAGE RISK

First North American Publication 1995.

The History of Hard Luck, Alaska

Hard Luck, situated fifty miles north of the Arctic Circle, near the Brooks Range, was founded by Adam O'Halloran and his wife, Anna, in 1931. Adam came to Alaska to make his fortune, but never found the gold strike he sought. Nevertheless, the O'Hallorans and their two young sons, Charles and David, stayed on—in part because of a tragedy that befell the family a few years later.

Other prospectors and adventurers began to move to Hard Luck, some of them bringing wives and children. The town became a stopping-off place for mail, equipment and supplies. The Fletcher family arrived in 1938 to open a dry goods store.

When World War II began, Hard Luck's population was fifty or sixty people, all told. Some of the younger men, including the O'Halloran sons, joined the armed services; Charles left for Europe in 1942, David in 1944 at the age of eighteen. Charles died during the fighting. Only David came home—with a young war bride, Ellen Sawyer (despite the fact that he'd become engaged to Catherine Fletcher shortly before going overseas).

After the war, David qualified as a bush pilot. He then built some small cabins to attract the sport fisherman and hunters who were starting to come to Alaska; he also worked as a guide. Eventually, in the early seventies, he built a lodge to replace the cabins—a lodge that later burned.

David and Ellen had three sons, born fairly late in their marriage—Charles (named after David's brother) was born in 1960, Sawyer in 1963 and Christian in 1965.

Hard Luck had been growing slowly all this time, and by 1970 it was home to just over a hundred people. These were the years of the oil boom, when the school and community center were built by the state. After Vietnam, ex-serviceman Ben Hamilton joined the community and opened the Hard Luck Café, which became the social focus for the town.

In the late 1980s, the three O'Halloran brothers formed a partnership, creating Midnight Sons, a bush-pilot service. They were awarded the mail contract, and also deliver fuel and other necessities to the interior. In addition, they serve as a small commuter airline, flying passengers to and from Fairbanks and within the North Arctic.

At the time these stories start, there are approximately 150 people living in Hard Luck—a preponderance of them male....

CHAPTER ONE

SO THIS WAS Hard Luck.

Lanni Caldwell slung her backpack over her shoulder, picked up her suitcase and crossed the gravel road that ran past the mobile office for Midnight Sons. The small airline—which served the Alaskan interior—had been mentioned in the news several times during the past week. Her curiosity piqued, Lanni had read the paper eagerly and watched the television reporters tell their tale. And what a tale it was. Midnight Sons had apparently spearheaded a campaign to attract women to Hard Luck with offers of jobs and housing.

Leave it to a bunch of lonely bush pilots to come up with such a crazy scheme! A number of single women had already arrived, and more would soon be joining them. TV reporters from down south were calling them "mail-order brides"—they weren't—and referring to Hard Luck as "the frozen north." It wasn't, at least not in June.

The sun shone bright and golden in a clear blue sky. The weather was in the comfortable seventies, with wildflowers blooming in a sassy array of colors that stretched from one end of the tundra to the other.

Lanni, who had grown up in Anchorage, had only been north of the Arctic Circle once before on a childhood visit to Hard Luck. But this all seemed familiar, because her grandmother, Catherine Fletcher, had often spoken of this town and her life here. Lanni could remember sitting on Grammy's knee as a child and listening to wondrous descriptions and exciting adventures, but those times with her grandmother had been few. Catherine's visits had come less and less often as the years progressed.

With Catherine's failing health, this might well be Lanni's last chance to learn about her grandmother's life on the tundra. It was the reason she'd agreed to spend her summer in Hard Luck. Beginning in September, she would become an intern at the Anchorage daily newspaper. After four years in college, her dream of working as a journalist was about to be realized. Lanni knew how fortunate she was to be chosen for the coveted position, and she was thrilled with the opportunity.

Her visit to Hard Luck had been prompted by a call from Sawyer O'Halloran to her mother, Kate, earlier in the month. Kate had seemed surprised to hear from one of the O'Hallorans, and even a bit annoyed. Lanni only vaguely understood why. She was aware of bad blood between her grandmother and the O'Hallorans, but she'd never really understood the reasons. It was something the family simply didn't talk about.

Sawyer O'Halloran had politely explained that with so many women moving into town, Hard Luck was in desperate need of housing. Catherine's home sat vacant, and Sawyer had asked if Kate would talk to her about renting it out.

Lanni wasn't entirely sure her mother had discussed the situation with Grammy. But Catherine Fletcher's health had worsened since her move to the nursing home in Anchorage, so perhaps it was best she hadn't been consulted.

"Hi." A young, freckle-faced boy smiled at her from atop his bicycle. A large, blue-eyed husky ambled along at his side. The dog's gaze quickly assessed Lanni as friend. He sat on his haunches, panting.

"Are you here for the wedding?" the boy asked.

"The wedding?" Lanni echoed.

"Yeah, my mom's marrying Sawyer O'Halloran. Lots of people are coming to Hard Luck for the wedding. Ben's making his special sweet-and-sour meatballs and everything. He said he'd let me and Susan roll some, too."

"Ben?"

"Yeah, he owns the Hard Luck Café. You're not a reporter or anything, are you?"

"No."

"It's a good thing, 'cause Sawyer said he wanted to kick their butts."

Lanni laughed. This didn't seem to be the time to announce that she was a journalism graduate. "I'm Lanni Caldwell."

"Scott Sutherland," he said, and grinned broadly, revealing front teeth too big for his mouth. "I bet you're the woman Sawyer's waiting for. He's been kind of frazzled lately."

No one had told Lanni she needed to check in with the O'Hallorans, but it couldn't hurt to introduce herself. After all, they were responsible for her being in town. She had reason to thank them, too. This summer was her one chance to explore some of the questions left unanswered by her family's official version of the past. There was so much she didn't know about Grammy, so many secrets, so many memories too painful to share. In many ways Lanni felt cheated out of part of her heritage, and it was because of this grandmother she barely knew.

"You want me to take you to meet Sawyer?" Scott asked.

"Sure." Lanni shifted her backpack and followed the boy to the mobile structure with Midnight Sons scrawled in bold red paint across the side.

"Sawyer," Scott called as he threw open the front door. The dog followed him inside. "Lanni Caldwell's here."

The man behind the desk looked up with a deep sigh of relief. "Thank heaven. Christian didn't think you'd arrive until after the wedding. You couldn't have picked a better time to show."

It was clear to Lanni, if no one else, that Sawyer O'Halloran had her confused with another person. Maybe he hadn't heard her surname.

"Listen," he went on, "I've got to get to a school-board meeting. I know it's a bit of a rush asking you to take over like this, but I can't very well sit around here answering the phones when I'm scheduled to chair a meeting at the school."

Lanni hedged, not sure what she should do. Sawyer seemed to think she was a secretary.

"If you have any questions, just write them down. I'll be back in an hour or two."

She opened her mouth to explain the mix-up when Sawyer bolted out the door. "I really appreciate this," he said as he flew past her.

"See what I mean?" Scott commented, flopping down in the chair Sawyer had just vacated. "You'd think he was gonna have a baby or something. Mom says she's never seen anything like it."

Lanni slipped the backpack from her shoulders and set it next to her suitcase. "Unfortunately he didn't give me a chance to tell him I'm not a secretary."

"You're not?"

Lanni slowly shook her head.

"You sure you don't have anything to do with those newspapers that've been bugging him?"

"I'm sure."

Scott relaxed visibly. "Why are you here then? Did Christian send you?"

"No. I'm here to clean out my grandmother's home so one or maybe two of the women will have somewhere to live."

"Christian didn't hire you?" This information obviously surprised the boy and he sat up straight. "I bet Charles didn't, either. He doesn't seem to think much of Sawyer and Christian's idea. He even offered to pay for my mom, my sister and me to fly back to Seattle. We almost did it, too, but Susan and I didn't want to go. Now," he said, and his face brightened, "Mom and Sawyer are getting married."

"You sound pleased about that."

"You bet. Sawyer's real neat. I never said anything to Mom, but I sorta missed having a dad. Sawyer's going to adopt me and Susan, and we're gonna be a real family."

"That's wonderful."

The phone rang just then. Lanni stared at it.

"Just answer 'Midnight Sons,'" Scott instructed, "and take a message."

Lanni reached for the receiver and did as Scott suggested.

"Sawyer won't be gone long," Scott stated confidently when she'd finished writing down the caller's information. "He'll probably end the meeting early." Scott cupped his hands behind his head, his thin elbows jutting out awkwardly. "He's so nervous about the wedding I wouldn't be surprised if he fainted right in front of the entire town before he can say I do." The image appeared to amuse Scott.

Lanni sat down at the desk across from the boy. "How many women have come to Hard Luck so far?" she asked.

"Not sure. A bunch, I guess. My mom was the first, though. Then there was this real pretty lady, but she didn't last long. Everyone said she wouldn't, and they were right. Christian was real disappointed when he found out she left. That was when he went through the applications again and hired another secretary. We thought you were her."

"That's an easy mistake to make."

"Dotty arrived last week. She's living with Mrs. Inman for now and learning all about running the health clinic. She's not young and pretty like my mom and you, but everyone's real glad she moved here. Mrs. Inman wants to go live with her daughter. She couldn't before because the town needed her to run the clinic."

"Well, I'm glad she can go to her daughter's now."

"If you want, I'll show you around later," Scott volunteered.

"Sure, why not?" It would help to have someone escort her about town. Lanni had been too young to remember that visit to Hard Luck more than twenty years before. It was much easier for Grammy to fly into Anchorage than for everyone else to make the long trek to Hard Luck. Besides, Kate Caldwell had never been close to her mother, and the years had only served to widen that gap.

"By the way, this is Eagle Catcher," Scott said, petting the husky's neck. "He was Sawyer's dog, but then Sawyer gave him to me. I've got the papers and everything."

"He's a beautiful dog."

"He likes you, too, and he doesn't like just anyone."

"I'm honored." Lanni ran her hand along the husky's thick coat. Before she could say anything further, the phone rang again. From that point on, her conversation with Scott was intermittent as she dealt with a variety of calls.

True to his word, Sawyer returned to the office in just over an hour. "I'm sorry to leave you so abruptly," he muttered, reading through his messages.

"Oh, it wasn't any problem," Lanni said breezily.

"Lanni isn't the new secretary," Scott announced, leaping out of Sawyer's chair.

Sawyer's expression went blank. "You're not?"

Lanni grinned, extending her hand. "I'm Lanni Caldwell. Catherine Fletcher's my grandmother." It might have been her imagination, but it seemed to Lanni that Sawyer's eyes hardened for just an instant.

"I see."

"I've come to clean out the house."

"You mean to say Catherine actually agreed to let us rent the place?"

"To be honest, I don't think my mother discussed it with her. My grandmother's in very poor health."

"I'm ... sorry to hear it."

Lanni wondered if that was true. The bad feelings between the two families clearly existed on both sides. Lanni wished she understood what had happened, and why. "I'd be willing to help out until your new secretary arrives," she offered, surprising herself. Someone needed to build a bridge of friendship, she supposed, and it might as well be her.

"You'd do that?" Sawyer eyed her speculatively, as if he wasn't sure he should trust her.

"I'd be happy to help out in any way I can," Lanni said with certainty. She had the impression she'd learn more about her grandmother working with the O'Halloran brothers than she ever would sorting and packing away Grammy's things.

"It'd only be now and again," Sawyer said hesitantly. "Until things settle down."

"Mom and Sawyer will be married in ten days," Scott piped in. "Not that I'm counting or anything."

"Then it's a deal." People said Lanni could charm a snake when she smiled, and she'd always considered her mouth her most attractive feature. It was full and classically shaped and expressive. Her teeth were even and white.

"You're sure you won't mind?" Sawyer asked, raking his fingers through his hair. "With Christian away, I'm shorthanded, and then the wedding... To top everything off, the school board needs to hire a new teacher."

"I'm happy to lend a hand," Lanni assured him again. "Really."

"It won't be for long. Christian'll be back soon. He's still in Seattle, but he'll be heading for British Columbia to visit our mother."

"If he isn't back soon," Scott added, "Sawyer said he was gonna throttle his scrawny neck."

Lanni laughed.

"Do you want me to carry your suitcase?" Scott asked.

"It's pretty heavy," Lanni cautioned.

"I may be skinny," Scott said with mock defiance, "but I'm strong."

"Uh, Lanni, would it be possible for you to come here tomorrow?" Sawyer's voice was casual, but she heard the eagerness behind it.

"What time would you like me?" she asked as she slid her arms into the backpack straps.

"Is eight too early?"

"Not at all. See you then."

"Thanks," he said, and he still seemed amazed by her willingness to assist him. "I mean that."

CHARLES O'HALLORAN stepped into the Midnight Sons office and glared at his brother. Not that it did any good. Sawyer had been in a world of his own from the moment Abbey Sutherland agreed to marry him.

Sawyer getting married.

Even now, Charles had difficulty accepting that his levelheaded brother was leaping into the abyss.

Charles had long accepted that Christian would probably marry someday, but not Sawyer. *Definitely* not Sawyer. Charles and Sawyer had both seen what could happen to two decent people when a marriage soured. They knew firsthand how the heartache spilled over into the lives of every family member. Charles wanted no part of that. He assumed Sawyer felt the same way.

From the moment he was old enough to leave home, Charles had struck out on his own. Following his high school graduation, he'd enlisted in the marines. Afterward he'd gone on to college, obtaining a degree in geology. Now he was a surveyor for Alaska Oil—the perfect job for him. He was often gone for weeks on end, searching for natural-gas deposits in the mineral-and gas-rich Alaskan interior.

"I'll have you know I talked with two reporters this afternoon," Charles muttered, making no effort to conceal his disgust. Not that he expected Sawyer to pay him any heed. His brother's head was so high in the clouds these days Charles suspected he was suffering from oxygen deprivation. That must be what had affected his thinking lately.

Sawyer stared at him blankly.

"They wanted to know about the women."

"There're only a few here," Sawyer said flatly, "and one of them is in her fifties."

"Yes, but the first one's getting married—practically before she had time to unpack her suitcase." It wasn't that Charles begrudged his brother happiness. What bothered him was, first, his distrust of the institution of marriage and, second, the fact that the town his grandparents had built was being turned into a national laughingstock.

"Did you tell them to take a flying leap into the nearest moose pile?"

Charles grinned despite his surly mood. "No, but I should've. What I did do was give them the number of the hotel where Christian's staying."

Sawyer nodded approvingly.

"I don't want you to get the wrong idea," Charles said, claiming a chair. "But frankly I don't think it was so smart to bring women to Hard Luck. The tabloids are having a field day with this. I read a headline this morning that was downright insulting."

"I don't care. I don't have a single regret."

Given Sawyer's present state of mind, Charles would've been shocked had he admitted to anything else.

"You're going to fall in love one day yourself," Sawyer said, eyeing him closely, "and then you'll know what I mean."

"God save me." Charles had managed to reach the age of thirty-five without getting snagged into a commitment, and he planned to continue the trend.

"Someday you're going to meet someone you'll really fall for," Sawyer said thoughtfully. "And I mean hard."

Charles gave a laugh. "Not me."

Sawyer's brows arched. "Sounds to me like you're tempting fate."

"Listen, I'm happy for you, Sawyer. You're obviously in love with Abbey and her kids, and I think that's wonderful—for you."

"But..."

"But I still don't condone what you and Christian did. It's a mistake to bring women to Hard Luck."

"Really?"

"You're damn right. Look at all the commotion the ones who've arrived have already caused. Just wait'll the day of the wedding. I bet you anything there'll be six or seven reporters here."

"Let 'em come," Sawyer said, seemingly unconcerned. "Inquiring minds want to know, and I say let 'em."

"You've got to be joking." Charles couldn't believe what he was hearing.

"I've got more important matters on my mind." Sawyer riffled through the papers on his desk and pulled out a packet of airline tickets. He kissed it, an expression of ecstasy on his face. "Two weeks in Hawaii—with my wife," he said, closing his eyes. "I can't imagine anything closer to heaven."

"What about the kids?"

Sawyer grinned. "Abbey's parents are going to take them to Disneyland. Later Abbey and I will meet them there and we'll all fly home together."

Charles couldn't really respond to his brother's enthusiasm for Hawaii. He'd seen all he wanted of the outside world. Nothing held the lure or the beauty he'd found in Alaska.

He'd let the others do the traveling. There wasn't anything he wanted that he couldn't find right here in Hard Luck. Their father and grandfather had felt the same way. Even when it might've saved his marriage, David O'Halloran hadn't been willing to move. As far as Charles was concerned, his father had made the only decision he could.

He realized as the thoughts swirled through his head how cold and hard they might seem. It wasn't that he didn't love his mother. He felt deeply protective of Ellen. He cared more than words could express for both his parents. He missed David still, with a grief that hadn't diminished in the years since his death. But he'd understood his father better than he ever would his delicate English mother.

"You look like you're thinking deep thoughts," Sawyer said, breaking into his musings.

"Not really," Charles muttered, not wanting to further the discussion with his younger brother. He stood up abruptly. "I just stopped by to tell you I've spent my day fending off the press."

"I appreciate it."

"But you should know nothing's going to stop them from attending the wedding."

Sawyer shrugged. "Then so be it."

If he lived to a hundred, Charles would never understand the changes he'd found in his brother the past few weeks.

STEPPING OUT of the trailer, Charles walked over to the Hard Luck Café, where Ben Hamilton served the freshest cup of coffee in town.

Charles slid onto a bar stool and turned the mug right side up.

Ben, who'd been a longtime friend and confidant, reached for the coffeepot. "Looks like you could use this."

"I could. Tell me something. Has everyone in this town gone crazy, or is it just me?"

"What are you talking about?"

"Bringing in the women, what else? I'm in Valdez minding my own business, having a pretty decent day. Then I open the newspaper, and lo and behold there's a picture of Sawyer—and another one of Christian. My own two brothers! There's this article about some screwball idea they've dreamed up—enticing women to move to Hard Luck."

"From what I understand, there're women in Anchorage who're upset Christian didn't take applications there."

"You've got to be joking!"

"That's what I heard," Ben said, leaning against the counter. "You want anything with that coffee?"

Charles shook his head, befuddled that the one person he'd expected to get a straight answer from was as caught up in this craziness as everyone else.

"Don't look so down in the mouth," Ben said. "It isn't as bad as it seems." The retired navy man—currently chief cook and bottle washer—returned to the kitchen, leaving Charles to stew in his discontent.

"By the way, did you see her?" Ben called out unexpectedly.

"See who?"

"The new gal who arrived in town. Pretty as a bug's ear. She's got long blond hair and a real cute nose. Young, though. Couldn't be more than twenty-two, twenty-three. Duke flew her in earlier. Scott took her over to the office. Looks like she's the new secretary Christian mentioned he'd hired. I wished we'd known she was coming. I would've baked a cake to welcome her. Seems all this town can think about these days is Sawyer and Abbey's wedding." He paused, rubbing the side of his jaw. "Fact is, I can't remember the last time there was a wedding here. Can you?"

"No," Charles barked, and slid off the stool. No matter where he went, he couldn't escape it. Even Ben had lost his grip on the real world. It was as if every male within a two-hundred-mile radius couldn't think about anything other than romance. They were all waiting for love to strike—but they didn't realize how undignified they'd look with Cupid's arrow sticking out of their rear ends!

"So you haven't met her?"

"No," Charles answered.

"Do you know where she's staying, then?"

"Haven't got a clue."

Ben frowned. "I hope someone thought to show her around. I'd hate for her to think we aren't hospitable."

In that case, Charles thought, he'd make a point of staying away from this latest arrival.

Still grumbling, he left the café. He walked toward his house, intent on finding a moment's privacy, when he heard someone call his name.

"Charles, look!"

He turned to find nine-year-old Scott Sutherland pumping away on an old bicycle that had belonged to Sawyer. Behind him, standing with her suitcase in the dirt, was a blond woman. No doubt the one Ben had mentioned.

The wind whipped her long hair about her face. She wore a sleeveless, pale blue summer dress. Not many women wore hats these days, but the straw one perched on her head, a bright yellow daisy attached to the front, suited her perfectly.

Eagle Catcher raced at Scott's side, barking.

Charles waved, fighting the urge to smile, and turned away.

"Wait up," Scott called. "You gotta meet Lanni."

Charles had no desire to be introduced to the latest example of his brothers' folly. He buried his hands in his pockets and increased his pace.

"Uncle Charles!"

That got to him. He was about to become an uncle—and he hadn't even realized it. Scott would soon be his nephew. He liked Scott, so the thought appealed to him. He turned back.

"Hello," Lanni said, walking toward them.

"Hello." Ben was right. She was a pretty thing. Her whole face seemed to sparkle. Her eyes were blue, their color enhanced by her dress. Her mouth was wide and expressive, curved in an expectant smile.

"Charles O'Halloran," he said, thrusting out his hand. The last thing he wanted was to be accused of staring.

She blinked once, then placed her hand in his. "Lanni Caldwell." She seemed to be waiting for him to say something more—yet she looked relieved when he didn't.

"It's nice to meet you, Charles."

"You, too." The full force of that smile was leveled on him. Charles frowned. He didn't like this sensation, whatever the hell it was. Nor was he keen on making small talk with a stranger.

"Mom's having Lanni over for dinner tonight," Scott announced. "Do you wanna come?"

Did he? Charles couldn't believe he was actually considering the invitation. "Sorry, I've got other plans," he muttered, before he could find a reason to change his mind.

"Mrs. Inman and Dotty'll be there."

"Sorry," he said again. "I wish I could." Charles managed to look disappointed, or so he thought until he caught the twinkle in Lanni's eye. She knew. She could see straight through him.

"If you don't come, I think Mom'll invite Duke," Scott said, sounding disappointed. "She left a message on your answering machine and asked you to call her back. Where've you been all afternoon?"

"Busy." This didn't seem the moment to announce that he'd spent most of the day fighting off the news media. Aside from his instinctive urge to stay away from Lanni Caldwell, the battle had left him in no mood for a dinner party. "Another time," he suggested. "Uh, see you around, Lanni."

"'Bye, Charles."

A couple of hours later, Charles regretted turning down the best invitation he'd had in weeks. Something must be wrong with him, only he had no idea what.

Wanting to kick himself, he decided to dine at Ben's. He walked out of the house just in time to see Duke strolling toward Christian's house, where Abbey and the kids were temporarily living. The bush pilot's hair was slickly combed into place, and he wore a clean shirt. Even from this distance, Charles could smell the other man's after-shave. Duke must have doused himself from head to foot with spice- and rum-scented cologne.

Charles found himself glaring at Duke as they made their way down opposite sides of the street. He was angry with the pilot for no reason he could name.

Ben generally served up a fairly decent meal, but Charles might've been eating sawdust for all the pleasure his spaghetti dinner gave him.

"You want another piece of garlic bread?" Ben asked.

"No, thanks."

"You don't seem to have much of an appetite this evening."

"I had a big lunch." It was a slight stretch of the truth.

"You interested in playing a little cribbage?" Ben asked.

Charles nodded. Wasting an hour or two with his old friend sounded a damn sight better than spending what remained of the evening alone wondering what was going on at his brother's house.

Before long, the two men faced each other across one of the small tables. Neither said much. Conversation wasn't really necessary when they sat down to play. They'd done this often enough through the years.

"You thinking about opening up the lodge?" Ben asked him out of the blue.

"The lodge? Why? What brings that up?" The lodge had once been the largest building in Hard Luck. It'd been filled with tourists eager to explore the Alaska interior. His father had owned and operated the business, but that, like so much else, had died with him.

Later a fire had destroyed part of the building. Repairing it now would be a costly, time-consuming affair. He hadn't the heart for it. Apparently Sawyer and Christian didn't, either, because neither one of them had mentioned anything about getting the place fixed up.

"It makes sense to open the lodge, doesn't it?" Ben persisted, moving his peg forward after counting his cards. "All the women moving into town—they need a decent place to live. Those cabins might work in the summer, but you can't honestly expect greenhorn women to last the winter there, can you?"

Charles wasn't going to even *think* about that. Where the "imported" women lived wasn't his concern. "Why don't you ask Sawyer or Christian what they intend to do?"

Ben looked directly at him, his expression as serious as Charles had ever seen it. "I'm asking you."

"Then you're asking the wrong guy. It wasn't me who enticed those women to move north. According to Christian, these gals all knew what they were getting themselves into. Far be it from me to interfere with my brothers' schemes."

"If you say so," Ben muttered.

Charles lost the game on a fluke. He had good card sense, and it wasn't like him to make stupid mistakes. He left soon afterward.

He was walking home when he saw Lanni Caldwell. He couldn't seem to take his eyes off her. She saw him, too, and her eyes rose to meet his. For an instant he was mesmerized by the warmth she exuded.

She smiled.

Without thinking, he smiled in return.

They stared at each other.

There was nothing coy in their exchange. Nothing flirtatious. She didn't blink or sweep her lashes downward or blush like a shy schoolgirl. He didn't bother to camouflage his interest.

Neither did she.

"Evening, Charles."

Duke Porter's voice caught him by surprise, and for the first time he noticed that Lanni wasn't alone.

"Evening," he said gruffly, and moved on. He passed them and had taken two, possibly three steps when he turned around.

At the same moment, Lanni cast a look over her shoulder and turned, too.

Once more their gazes met. And held.

As if she felt the urgent need to escape, Lanni whirled around and hurried to catch up with Duke.

With his heart in his throat, Charles walked straight past his own house and continued until he reached Christian's. Abbey and the kids were living there until after the wedding. Sawyer stood on the front porch, wearing a cocky grin.

"All right," Charles said with ill grace. "Tell me about her."

CHAPTER TWO

"WHO AM I SUPPOSED to tell you about?" Sawyer asked.

Charles hated the smug look on his brother's face. Sawyer was going to make him suffer before giving him the information he wanted.

"You know who I mean!" Charles barked.

"You don't by any chance mean Lanni Caldwell, do you?"

"Yes," Charles snapped, "I do."

Striking a casual pose, Sawyer leaned against the porch railing and folded his arms. He was clearly enjoying this far more than necessary. "What do you want to know?"

"First off, what's she doing in Hard Luck?"

Sawyer considered the question longer than necessary. "For the moment she's working as my secretary."

Charles didn't question the "for the moment" part. "She's not staying in one of those dilapidated cabins, is she?"

"No. As a matter of fact, Catherine Fletcher has agreed to let us rent her house. Lanni's living there."

That was a relief. Those pitiful excuses for cabins hadn't been used in years. Charles knew that his brothers and their crew of bush pilots, as well as some of the townsfolk, had worked hard to clean up the old hunting cabins. Nevertheless, Charles didn't like the idea of

Lanni—or anyone else—living in them. Furthermore, he didn't want Lanni sleeping outside of town, away from everything and everyone, especially on her first night. People seemed to conveniently forget there were dangers lurking about, especially to someone unfamiliar with life north of the Arctic Circle.

"Are you saying you're...romantically interested in Lanni?" Sawyer asked in the smooth easy drawl he used when he knew he had the upper hand. "You don't realize..."

"Realize what?"

"Never mind." Sawyer wore the cocky look that always irritated Charles—the look that meant he knew something his brother didn't. Charles refused to play his game.

"You're attracted to Lanni," Sawyer said now. "Remember what I told you about tempting the fates? I love it. I absolutely love it."

Charles gave a short, derisive laugh. "How could I be attracted to the woman? I don't even know her. I only want to make sure nothing happens to her. The last thing we need is more bad press."

"You weren't this concerned when you first met Abbey."

"Sure I was," Charles said defensively. "I offered her airfare home, didn't I? I was worried about her and the kids—the same way I'm worried about what's going to happen to Lanni...whatever her name is."

Sawyer lowered his head in an unsuccessful attempt to hide a knowing grin. Charles hated to think his brother could read him that easily. Apparently his interest in Lanni was as clear as glacial runoff.

"Lanni's a sweet kid," Charles added, trying to explain his concern. He feared, however, that he was only digging himself in deeper. "Like I told you," he insisted, "I don't want to see anything happen to her."

"She's not a child, Charles. She's a woman."

Remembering the almost dizzying sense of attraction he'd experienced moments earlier, Charles didn't need to be reminded of that.

"Do you think it's a good idea for Duke to be walking her home?" he asked a little anxiously.

Sawyer laughed outright. "She'll be fine."

Charles let his gaze follow the road to the point where he'd last seen Lanni. It wasn't *entirely* that he didn't trust Duke Porter to mind his manners. His main objection, he had to admit, was that Lanni was spending time with another man.

Something was wrong. Very wrong. Charles barely knew Lanni, and he was damn near having a jealous fit because someone else had walked her home. He'd better leave before he managed to make a world-class fool of himself over a woman who was really just a stranger. And too young for him, besides.

"I'll talk to you in the morning," Charles told his brother abruptly. He stepped off the porch and made it all the way to the gate before Sawyer called to him.

"There's more to Lanni Caldwell than meets the eye."

Charles said nothing, although he'd already decided the same thing for himself.

"She's intelligent and witty and has a wonderful heart."

"A wonderful heart" was an expression their grandmother had used. He'd almost forgotten it. Anna O'Halloran had a talent for seeing the good in others. She'd always described those who were by nature generous and caring as having a wonderful heart. Perhaps that was what Charles had sensed when he met Lanni. Her wonderful heart.

"I wish you'd cancelled your plans and joined us for dinner," Sawyer added.

Sawyer wasn't the only one who regretted that decision. Charles nodded, which was all the admission he was willing to make. Once again he started for his own home.

"Charles?"

Sighing, he turned back.

Sawyer was grinning. "Are you going to offer Lanni Caldwell airfare home?"

ABBEY SUTHERLAND joined her husband-to-be on the front porch. He slipped his arm around her waist and bent down to kiss. Even now, it didn't seem possible that she and Sawyer could be together like this. They'd come so close to losing each other.

"Was that Charles I heard you talking to?" she asked.

Sawyer frowned as he answered her with a distracted nod. "He met Lanni. He doesn't know she's related to Catherine. I should've told him, but I want my brother to see her for herself. I want him to judge her as the woman she is, rather than as a member of the family that brought so much pain to ours."

Abbey rested her cheek against his chest. "It was more than that, wasn't it?"

He rubbed his hand down the length of Abbey's arm. "I like Lanni."

"Does that surprise you?"

"Yes," he admitted, "in a way it does."

"She's not a monster."

"I know," Sawyer agreed quickly. "It's just that I find it hard to believe someone as *nice* as Lanni Caldwell could be related to Catherine Fletcher." Then, almost in afterthought, he said, "My diehard bachelor brother is attracted to her. He's having enough trouble owning up to that. If he found out about Lanni's relationship to Catherine, his interest would shrivel up and die. I don't want that to happen. I have a feeling Lanni's just the one to teach my arrogant brother a lesson or two."

Abbey grinned, lifting her head to look up into Sawyer's clear, blue-gray eyes. "Charles vulnerable to a woman—my, my. I can't imagine who that sounds like, can you?" she asked, her voice warm with teasing.

"As far as I'm concerned, falling in love could only do Charles good. But I wish . . ."

"You wish the woman was someone who's not related to Catherine Fletcher."

"Exactly," Sawyer muttered.

ALTHOUGH IT WAS past midnight, Lanni couldn't sleep. She'd have blamed the sunlight if she hadn't been born and raised in Anchorage. The midnight sun was nothing new to her.

Filled with nervous energy, she showered and changed into her favorite loose-fitting pajamas, then brewed herself a small pot of tea. She moved into her grandmother's living room and sat on the couch with her legs folded under her, then took a tentative sip of the steaming tea. Across from her, on top of the ancient television, sat two framed photographs. High school graduation photos. One was of Matt, her older brother, and the other was of herself.

Seeing the photographs comforted Lanni. It made her feel less . . . guilty about moving into her grandmother's house. Less if she were invading her privacy. Catherine had suffered a slight stroke several months earlier. She hadn't wanted to move into the Anchorage nursing facility and had always intended to return home to Hard Luck. Even now, she considered her stay in Anchorage temporary. Grammy didn't seem to realize she wasn't getting better. Perhaps that was a blessing.

Lanni glanced at the photograph again. Her grandmother loved her and Matt enough to display their pictures to anyone who came into her home. But that fact led to a hundred other questions. Why had Catherine never shown any real pride or interest in her grandchildren? Why had she hidden her feelings from them? Lanni found it incredibly sad that Catherine had such a difficult time showing affection. She knew her own mother had often felt cheated and hurt by the things Catherine had said and done. Yet Kate Caldwell had cared tenderly for her mother over the months following Catherine's stroke.

Not wanting to dwell on the problems confronting her mother and grandmother in Anchorage, Lanni studied her brother's youthful face, instead. She was worried about him, especially since his divorce from Karen.

Lanni longed to shake some sense into both her brother and his ex-wife. She refused to believe that two people who loved each other so deeply would allow their marriage to fall apart.

But if she was going to blame anyone, it would be Matt. At thirty, he was five years older than Lanni— and about five years younger in attitude. Matt couldn't make a decision about what he wanted to do with his life. Throughout his marriage, he'd drifted from one area of interest to another, uprooting Karen every time. He'd tried his hand at accounting, commercial fishing, and perhaps most interesting, he'd attended cooking school.

Six months into each venture, just when Karen had readjusted her life, Matt decided this new interest wasn't what he wanted, after all.

She didn't think her brother was irresponsible or reckless, but his driving need for change and his general dissatisfaction with life had led to the breakup of his marriage.

Lanni forced her thoughts away from Matt. It was after midnight—she should be sound asleep. Her day had started in the wee hours of the previous morning, and she was exhausted.

Unbidden, the image of Charles O'Halloran's face drifted into her mind. Their meeting on the road that evening had been the oddest thing. Attraction—an attraction unlike any she'd ever experienced—had charged the air between them.

Somehow, as if by a magical touch, Lanni had known what Charles was feeling, because she'd felt the same bewildering round of sensations herself.

Had she not been with Duke, Lanni feared she would have closed the distance that separated them and walked directly into Charles's arms.

He would have welcomed her, too. Of that Lanni was certain.

Perhaps it was the lure of the forbidden. The grass-is-greener syndrome. Wanting what you know you can't have. Lanni wished she'd paid more attention in her psychology classes. Charles was an O'Halloran. An enemy of her family—except that Lanni didn't know the reasons for their enmity. Perhaps she was doing something terribly disloyal by dining with members of his family.

But Charles hadn't been there for dinner.

Technically Sawyer hadn't invited her, either. It was Abbey who'd insisted she come. Over the meal and the conversation that followed, no mention was made of the problems between the O'Hallorans and the Fletchers.

She would phone her mother, Lanni decided, and this time she'd insist on some answers. She had a right to know. A right to make her own decisions and choices.

It didn't help that she was so strongly attracted to Charles O'Halloran. She didn't understand why, but she felt almost a spiritual link with this man. She felt what she could only describe as a sense of destiny, of fate, when she was near him—and that was something she wasn't even sure she believed in!

Lanni stayed awake until her head felt heavy and her eyelids stung. She slipped between the clean sheets and cradled the thick feather pillow. Closing her eyes, she walked mentally through each room of the house. It should only take her a couple of weeks to pack everything and arrange to have it delivered to Anchorage. She planned to start with Catherine's bedroom. Perhaps she'd find something there that would help her piece together why the O'Hallorans so adamantly disliked her family... and why her family felt the same way.

CHARLES SPENT the first part of his morning on the phone doing his damnedest to keep busy. He didn't want to think about his brothers' new secretary. Yet time and again he found his mind wandering down to the mobile office next to the runway. Lanni was sure to stir up interest among the pilots. He tightened his jaw, knowing that John, Ralph, Duke and the rest would be falling all over each other in an effort to court her.

He could picture them gathering around her desk, disturbing her while she worked. They'd be telling her stories and making her laugh, and generally acting like fools.

Well, Charles wasn't going to join them. *He* wasn't willing to play the fool over a woman, no matter who she was. At least that was what he repeatedly told himself.

By ten o'clock Charles had had a change of heart. He grabbed a light sweater and headed briskly out the front door.

"Morning," Pete Livengood, the proprietor of the grocery store, called out as he walked past.

"Morning," Charles answered, wondering if Pete had heard about Lanni's arrival. From Sawyer's stories, he understood that Pete had taken an instant liking to Abbey and proposed practically within the first five minutes of meeting her. He smiled at the memory of Sawyer's outrage over their friend's interest.

Then Charles thought of Lanni and wondered if the old coot had proposed marriage—or anything else—to her. Involuntarily his hands tightened into fists. There'd be hell to pay if he had.

The green-eyed monster had struck again, Charles realized.

As he stepped up to the mobile, he felt his heart kick into high gear. He didn't have much of an excuse for stopping by. Although he was a partner in the air service with Sawyer and Christian, his role was more of a silent one. They rarely consulted him on business decisions—and they sure hadn't consulted him before embarking on this latest scheme!

He walked into the office to discover Lanni sitting behind a desk typing. Her long hair was pulled back from her face and fastened with a clip at the base of her neck. Her eyes widened when she saw him and her hands froze over the keyboard.

"Hello again," he said, attempting to look as though he had an important reason for being there. "Is Sawyer around?"

"He took a flight this morning. One of the pilots—John, I think he said his name is—came down with a flu bug. Sawyer said he'd be back around one or so."

Charles immediately wondered if John's flu bug had been a way to get Sawyer out of the office so he could make time with Lanni. John Henderson had made a point of letting Charles know where he stood on the issue of bringing women to Hard Luck. Either women came to live here or he was moving on to another air service.

This was a familiar complaint among the pilots, Charles knew, especially in the bleak, dark months of winter. He didn't understand why Christian and Sawyer had given in to what amounted to blackmail, but then, he reminded himself, he wasn't making the decisions. Obviously.

"Is there something you'd like me to tell Sawyer when he returns?" she asked, reaching for a message pad and pen. For the life of him, Charles couldn't come up with a single thing to say to his brother.

"I'll talk to him later," he said on a decisive note. "Thanks, anyway."

"I'll leave a message for Sawyer that you stopped by."

Charles shoved his hands into his pockets. "Great."

He hesitated. His heart felt as if it was leaping and dancing inside his chest. "I don't suppose you've ever gone panning for gold, have you?"

Her eyes revealed her interest. "No. No, I haven't."

"My grandfather's claim is still active, and I was thinking I'd take a trip up there this afternoon. I was wondering if you'd, uh, like to come along and see how it's done, that is, of course, if, uh—"

She nodded even before he'd finished. "I'd love to. What time are you leaving?"

Charles had to think fast. "Any time is fine. Whenever you you can get away from here, just let me know."

"Sawyer will be back soon, I'm sure."

"Good," he said, doing his best to hide his delight. "Give me a call when you're ready."

Charles thought her smile could melt the polar ice cap. "Thank you for asking me, Charles."

Thank you for asking me. Charles hardly dared to believe she'd actually agreed. It was all he could do to keep from clicking his heels as he walked out of the office.

Whatever it was, he had it bad. *Real* bad.

Charles hurried to the house and gathered together his supplies. Within half an hour he'd loaded the back of his pickup. Now all he had to do was wait for Lanni's call.

"Where are you going?" Scott asked as he rode up on his bicycle.

"To the gold claim my grandfather used to mine," Charles explained. He tucked a second shovel in the bed of his truck. There were probably any number of shovels available at the site, but he wanted to be sure. He'd also found himself packing things that had nothing to do with gold mining: a bottle of wine, a loaf of sour-dough bread and a hunk of cheddar cheese.

"Can I come?"

"Another time, Scott," Charles replied absently, checking to see if he'd forgotten anything.

"Promise?"

"Promise," Charles said, smiling. "We'll bring your sister, too."

"No girls," Scott protested. "Why do women have to ruin everything?"

A day earlier, Charles would have agreed with the boy, but not now. Within an hour or two, Lanni would be joining him, and frankly nothing could have pleased Charles more.

"Susan wants to ride my bike," Scott complained. "I don't want her to, 'cause if I let her and she learns how, she'll want it all the time." He glanced over his shoulder and groaned. "Here she comes now."

The little girl raced toward Scott. "You said I could ride your bike," she said in an accusing voice. She planted her hands on her hips, as if daring her older brother to refuse her.

"You don't know how," Scott insisted.

"Everyone has to learn sometime. Mom said you had to let me, remember?"

"All right, all right," Scott muttered, climbing off with a decided lack of enthusiasm. He cast Charles a forlorn look as he handed over the bike.

"Besides, I know how to ride a bike," Susan said righteously. "A little, anyway."

"The seat's too high and you can't reach the pedals and—"

"I can too reach the pedals."

The argument sounded like one that had been repeated often. Charles grinned as he watched the brother and sister engage in verbal battle. It didn't seem all that many years ago that he and Sawyer had fought over whose turn it was to ride the bike. Their parents had settled the issue by buying Sawyer his own bike for Christmas. The very one Scott had reluctantly passed over to his sister.

The boy climbed onto the back of Charles's truck and sat on the tailgate. "I don't want to watch," he said. "She's probably going to wreck the best bike I ever had, and all because she's a girl."

"Be patient," Charles advised the boy under his breath. "The harder you resist, the more attractive the bike will be to her. Women always want what they can't have."

"What about men?"

"Well, we're the same—but not as bad." Then, in afterthought, he added, "Don't tell your mother I said that. She might not understand. All right?" He didn't want a war with his soon-to-be sister-in-law.

"All right," Scott whispered.

With Charles's help, Susan climbed onto the bicycle. Her toes barely reached the pedals, even after Charles had lowered the seat as far as it would go. She looked up and beamed him a radiant smile of triumph.

"Thanks, Uncle Charles."

Being called uncle would take some getting used to, but as Charles had realized the day before, he rather liked it.

"I'll walk beside you until you get going," Charles promised.

Scott got to his feet. "Just make sure she doesn't crash!" he shouted.

Susan started peddling, and the bike wobbled precariously from side to side. Charles trotted along beside her until she found her balance, then he stopped and waited breathlessly for Susan to ride away on her own.

"She's doing all right," Scott muttered, adding, "for a girl."

"She's doing great." Charles felt a surge of pride as if he alone was responsible for Susan's success. He continued to watch as the seven-year-old turned the bike around and rode back.

"She shouldn't get so close to the side of the road," Scott warned. "There's all kinds of rocks there."

Charles was about to call out a warning when Susan made the unpleasant discovery for herself. The bicycle wobbled, then crashed into the bushes. Almost immediately they heard her howl of pain.

Scott leapt out of the truck and darted down the road toward his sister, with Charles following. When they reached Susan, Charles carefully pulled the bike away and handed it to Scott, who inspected the wheel to make sure it wasn't bent.

"Are you okay?" Charles asked as he gently helped the child from the bushes. Tears streaked her face, and her small shoulders jerked as she struggled to hold in her sobs.

Susan sat by the side of the road and twisted her arm so she could look at her elbow. "Here," she said, showing him the scraped skin. "Here, too." She pushed up the leg of her pants to examine her knee.

"You'd better let me wash that off and put on some disinfectant."

"It's not the kind that stings, is it?" Scott asked, sounding concerned. He stood over Charles and studied his sister's injuries.

"No," Charles said. "It isn't the kind that stings."

He carried Susan back and sat her on the tailgate, then hurried into the house for the necessary first-aid supplies. Although she didn't really need them, he brought out a couple of Band-Aids.

The little girl grimaced as he cleaned the scrapes and gritted her teeth when he sprayed on the disinfectant. She released a slow smile and announced, "It didn't hurt."

"I told you it wouldn't," Charles said with an answering smile. He carefully placed the two small adhesive strips on her knee and elbow, then he helped her down.

Before Susan's feet reached the ground, she wrapped her arms around his neck and hugged him tight. "Thank you, Uncle Charles." With that, she was off like a shot, racing as fast as her legs would carry her toward the library. Scott hopped on his bike and rode after her, with a grateful wave and a "See you later" for Charles.

Watching them go, Charles felt his heart constrict. Sawyer was a lucky man, he thought. Not only had he fallen in love with Abbey, but she was bringing the priceless gift of her children to their marriage.

Back in the house, the phone rang. It was Lanni. Sawyer had returned and she was free to leave the office. Charles picked her up at Catherine Fletcher's house, and before long, she was sitting beside him in the cab of his truck. Feeling more lightheaded than he had in years, he headed north on the maintenance road that headed out of Hard Luck.

"You said your grandfather used to mine this claim?" she asked conversationally.

He was pleased to note that she'd changed clothes and was dressed appropriately in blue jeans, a long-sleeved shirt and ankle-high boots. He'd brought along bug spray to ward off the mosquitoes, but unfortunately that went only so far in keeping the pesky critters away.

"My grandfather, Adam, and his wife, Anna, settled Hard Luck in the early 1930s. Like thousands of men and women before them, they came in search of a dream." He didn't mean to sound poetic, but he'd heard the story so often he found himself repeating it just the way his grandmother used to tell it. "The gold dredges working near Fairbanks were digging up huge quantities of gold. I don't recall the precise amount," he said, "but one dredge in a four- or five-year span was responsible for more than ten million dollars' worth of gold, and that was when the price was thirty-five dollars an ounce."

"That's enough to keep someone content, you'd think."

"My grandfather got hit with gold fever while working on a dredge. But he was convinced the motherlode lay north. He planned to strike it rich someday."

"Did he?"

Charles sighed. "Not in the way he wanted or expected. He found some gold but never discovered the huge vein he sought. He found something else, something far more valuable, though. He built a town and settled a land. He created a community that's grown and thrived. Without meaning to, my grandfather shaped the lives of several generations." Charles paused, wondering how much more he should say. "I believe the gold's there—the major strike he was hoping to discover. But now it'll be one of Adam's descendants who finds it.''

The maintenance road ended, and Charles slowed as they crossed the rugged tundra. The ride was far less smooth now. The track, what there was of it, was barely recognizable, even to him. But then, he only visited the site two or three times a year.

Soon Lanni could hear the sound of rushing water. She glanced at Charles questioningly.

"That's the Koyukuk River," he explained.

"Koyukuk," Lanni repeated. "It sounds like you're trying to clear your throat."

Charles laughed. "It's an Athabascan word, I believe. Although you've probably never heard of it, the Koyukuk is the third longest river in Alaska. It stretches over 550 miles."

"Then the longest must be the Yukon?"

"Right, but it covers three times the territory."

"That *is* impressive."

Charles threw her a look. He had the feeling she already knew this. "An Indian friend of mine lives close by. I hope you don't mind if we drop in," he said. "Fred's a trapper, and I haven't seen him in some time."

"That'd be fine," Lanni assured him.

Charles smiled at her. Being with Lanni felt completely natural. When he'd first spoken to her that morning, his mouth had been so dry he could barely speak. Not now.

Soon they approached Fred Susitna's cabin, a weathered log structure nestled among scrub trees. A tin-covered porch extended halfway across the front, and a row of lanterns hung from hooks along the roof edge.

Charles had no sooner turned off the engine when Fred appeared. His tanned, leathery face broke into a wide grin of welcome. Charles had been making impromptu visits to Fred's cabin for years, and his friend never seemed to age. Fred could be forty or sixty, Charles didn't know.

"Welcome, my friend," Fred said, and hugged him as if it had been ten years since his last visit, instead of ten months. He slapped Charles on the back, then turned to meet Lanni.

"Fred Susitna, this is Lanni Caldwell."

The trapper greeted her as he had Charles, with a hug of welcome. He ushered them into his home and went about heating oil to fry bread. It was a custom to feed visitors in the Alaskan interior.

Within minutes they were served hot coffee and deep-fried bread coated with granulated sugar. Charles watched as Lanni finished the warm bread and licked the sugar from her fingertips.

His friend murmured something in Athabascan. Although Charles didn't understand the words Fred spoke, their meaning was clear.

Charles could feel the blood heat in his ears.

He managed to make small talk for a while, asking about the line Fred trapped each winter. Lanni was full of questions when Fred proudly brought out and showed her the furs.

It didn't take Charles long to realize it had been a mistake to bring Lanni to meet Fred. Not because of her questions, but because his friend saw through him far too easily. As soon as he could do so without rudeness, Charles made an excuse to leave.

"It was good to see you again," he said, edging his way to the door.

"It is always a pleasure," Fred said, walking out to the truck with him. "Come again soon and bring your woman."

He waited for Lanni to deny that she belonged to him or any other man. Women seemed to have a thing about that these days.

"Lanni isn't my woman," Charles corrected when she didn't say anything.

"No?" Fred Susitna asked, dark eyes twinkling. "I've never seen you run from the truth before, my friend."

If Lanni heard the Indian's remarks, she didn't comment, and Charles was grateful.

The old mining site was less than five miles down the river. Charles parked the truck and helped Lanni out. Gazing around her, she walked over to the shore of the Koyukuk River. The water rushed past like a roaring freight train, drowning out every other sound.

When Charles came to stand by her side, she turned and smiled up at him, a sense of excitement and pure rapture at the river's fierce power. He swore he didn't mean to kiss her. It just happened. One minute he was thinking how lovely she looked, how ... kissable her mouth seemed, and the next she was in his arms.

What started out as something unexpected, a moment's gratification, quickly became much more. They kissed again and again, tenderly, then heatedly; gently, then with a restless hunger that left him breathless and confused.

He needed to read what was in her eyes. He had to know what she was thinking, but discovered he was afraid to ask. He eased his mouth from hers and searched her beautiful deep blue eyes. What he found there gave him pause.

"Lanni," he whispered, shocked by the tenderness he saw, the acceptance.

"Have we both gone crazy?" she asked him, whispering despite their solitude.

"We must have."

They kissed again, a lazy, sensuous kiss, and when they broke apart, Charles was trembling. Trembling. Charles O'Halloran, ever calm and unemotional. Ever sensible and prudent. The man who'd been so sure where he stood when it came to falling in love.

Only the day before, his brother had suggested he was tempting the fates. And now the fates had sent Lanni into his life to teach him a well-deserved lesson.

"I . . . I need to sit down," Lanni said.

Charles could barely hear her above the sound of the rushing water. If truth be known, his own legs weren't too steady, either. He slid an arm around Lanni, and together they leaned against a boulder; he caught his breath and let his heartbeat slow down.

Charles considered apologizing—except that he wasn't sorry. Instead, he tightened his arm, and she snuggled against him. He looked into incredibly blue eyes filled with promise.

"Charles, there's something—"

Unable to resist her a moment longer, he brought his lips down to brush hers.

She moaned softly, the sound mingled with a tantalizing sigh of pleasure. "I should tell you—"

"Whatever it is, it doesn't matter. Only this does." He kissed her again, deciding that if this was craziness, it was the most wonderful feeling he'd ever experienced.

"We came for gold," she reminded him when she could speak again.

"I've already found it," Charles said, and kissed her once more.

CHAPTER THREE

LANNI'S HAND SHOOK as she dialed the number of her family home. Her father answered on the second ring.

"Hi, Dad," she said cheerfully.

"Lanni, it's good to hear from you. How's everything in Hard Luck?"

"Just great."

"Your mother wishes she could've come up with you. But we've already been over that—she's needed here, and it made sense for you to be the one to clear out your grandmother's house."

"Speaking of Mom, is she there? I need to talk to her."

"I'm sorry, sweetheart, she's at the nursing home with your grandmother."

"Oh." It was difficult to keep the disappointment out of her voice.

"Is there anything I can help you with?"

Lanni bit her lower lip. "It has to do with the O'Halloran family." Before she could say anything more, her father interrupted.

"Are they bothering you? You might remind those troublemakers that *we're* the ones doing *them* the favor. The least they could do is be cooperative."

"Daddy, they are! They've been fantastic. Sawyer and his fiancée had me over for dinner last night, and Charles—he's the oldest brother—took me out to his grandfather's gold stake this afternoon.'' She didn't say that they'd never gotten around to panning for gold the way they'd intended. The afternoon had been spent touring the campsite and sipping wine over a camp stove and talking for hours on end. She'd told him about her studies at the University of Washington and her dreams of being a writer. Although she'd known it was deceptive, she didn't mention her grandmother. She talked about her brother, though, and confessed how worried she was about him.

Her father hesitated. "Well, I'm glad to hear they've made you feel welcome."

"I need to know what the old feud is all about, Dad. All I can remember is the little bit Mom told me."

"It's not important anymore, sweetheart," her father insisted. "It all happened a long time ago and it's best forgotten."

"But I'm dealing with the O'Hallorans now! I need to know what happened."

Her father was silent a moment. Finally he said, "I think this is something you should discuss with your mother. If you want, I'll have her phone you later."

"Please do."

They chatted a little longer, then said their goodbyes. Disappointed that she was still left in the dark, Lanni made herself a sandwich and wandered into her grandmother's bedroom.

The bulky headboard and matching dresser dated from the forties. The meticulously kept room told Lanni little about Catherine's life.

She started with the closet and emptied the contents onto the bed. A row of shoe boxes lined the top shelf. As she brought them down, Lanni realized that not all of the boxes contained shoes. A peek inside one revealed several orderly stacks of black-and-white photographs.

Taking the box with her, Lanni moved into the kitchen and sat down at the table. The first pile of photos was of her mother as a child. Lanni smiled as she saw her mother's toddler face glaring into the camera from the top of a snowbank outside the house. Grammy and the grandfather who'd died before she was born looked on.

From what Lanni knew of her family history, her grandparents had divorced shortly after those photos were taken. Their daughter, Kate, Lanni's mother, had been much closer to her father, Willie, than to Catherine. Willie Fletcher had moved to Anchorage, and Kate had lived with him there, occasionally visiting her mother for a few weeks at a time. Catherine Fletcher had steadfastly refused to leave Hard Luck, even when it meant giving up custody of her only child.

Most of the photographs were of people Lanni didn't recognize. She found a few from her grandmother's wedding to William Fletcher. Catherine wore a lovely pastel-colored suit and held a small bouquet of white rosebuds.

Lanni spread the photos across the table and carefully examined each picture, searching for an answer. None revealed itself. When she'd finished, she placed the snapshots back inside the shoe box and returned it to the bedroom.

It was when she emptied the drawers that Lanni found the faded manila envelope. Sitting on the edge of the bed, she opened the metal tab and pulled out an eight-by-ten professionally taken photograph of her grandmother. Catherine couldn't have been more than twenty. Her eyes were bright with happiness, and a gentle smile softened her face. Scrawled across the top of the picture were the words "To My Darling David." At the bottom was "Remember me, Love Always, Catherine."

David.

Lanni couldn't remember anyone ever mentioning a David. The second photo revealed her grandmother in a long, flowing white wedding dress with a satin train that circled her feet. She turned the picture over to find the address of a Fairbanks photographer stamped on the back.

Her grandmother had married twice? Lanni had already examined the pictures of her grandparents' wedding, and Catherine had worn a pastel suit. There'd been no white wedding dress and traditional veil.

The phone rang just then, and Lanni leapt up to answer it. "Hello?"

"Sweetheart, your father said you called. Is everything all right?"

"Everything's fine." Only it wasn't, not really. Her heart pounded as if she'd stumbled upon something she was never meant to discover. "I called because I wanted to find out what I could about the feud with the O'Hallorans."

"That's what your father said. I don't think there'd be any harm in telling you." Her mother hesitated, perhaps unsure where she should start. "More than fifty years ago, your grandmother was engaged to David O'Halloran."

"They were engaged," Lanni whispered, looking down at the photo in her hands.

"Unfortunately World War II got in the way of their wedding. My mother wanted to marry before David was shipped to England, but with such an uncertain future, David preferred that they wait.

"Mom lived for David's letters. She wrote him each and every day. According to what she told me, they were very much in love. She even had her wedding dress made and her photograph taken and sent to him."

That explained the picture.

"Then Charles—David's elder brother—was killed in France. The two were very close, and for three months afterward, Catherine didn't receive a single letter from David. She was frantic until finally word arrived that David was coming home. But he didn't arrive alone. He came with an English bride—Ellen."

"Oh, no." Lanni closed her eyes, feeling her grandmother's pain and rejection as if it were her own.

"It seems that when David learned of his brother's death, he was inconsolable. He tried to explain his feelings to my mother, but Catherine wouldn't listen. She didn't want to hear that this young, beautiful Englishwoman had helped him through his grief.

"Apparently Ellen's family had died in the war, and she and David were both lost, lonely people. I suppose it's understandable that they'd fall in love."

"Poor Grammy," Lanni whispered.

"You see, Lanni, your grandmother never loved another man. I'm not really sure why she married my father. She never loved him, never wanted him. It was always David O'Halloran. She pined for him all her life. When he died, it was as if she lost her reason for living."

"Oh, Mom, what a sad story." It helped explain so many things. No wonder her mother and grandmother had never been close. Kate was the product of a marriage to a man her grandmother had never loved. And her mother had always known that.

"It would have been much better if it was David who'd died in the war, instead of Charles," Kate said in a low, harsh voice.

Lanni's heart clenched at the words. If David had died, there would have been no sons. No Sawyer. No Christian. *No Charles*.

"Naturally I don't know everything that happened after David brought Ellen home with him," Kate went on, sounding almost normal again. "Knowing my mother, she didn't do anything to make Ellen feel welcome. I'm sure the town's sympathy went to Catherine, and I'm also sure she took full advantage of that. Knowing her, I'm fairly certain she made Ellen's life as miserable as her own."

"Why would she stay in Hard Luck?" Lanni asked. It must have been torture for Catherine to watch the man she loved with another woman.

"I can't answer that. I believe Mother lived with the hope that David and Ellen would eventually divorce. I understand there were problems with the marriage from the first. And my mother was there on the sidelines— patiently waiting for David to leave Ellen. Only he never did."

"She never stopped loving him," Lanni murmured.

"Or hating him," Kate added. "I believe there was a fine line between love and hate as far as my mother and David O'Halloran were concerned."

"I've met two of his sons. The oldest is Charles— they probably named him after the Charles who died in the war. Sawyer's the middle one. His wedding is at the end of next week—he's marrying one of the women who answered the newspaper ad. They seem very much in love."

"It certainly didn't take him long."

"Charles claims Sawyer barely gave Abbey time to unpack her suitcase. I didn't know two people could fall in love so quickly. It was as if they knew from the moment they met that they were meant to be together."

"It happens like that sometimes."

"Abbey's got two children from a previous marriage. Seeing the four of them together, you'd never know Sawyer wasn't their father. Whatever they have is special, and they know it."

"I'm happy for him," her mother said, but she sounded distracted. "You won't stay there longer than necessary, will you?"

"No," Lanni replied, but she knew what her mother was thinking. She was worried that Lanni, too, would be swept off her feet. She opened her mouth to reassure Kate, then abruptly closed it.

She wasn't entirely certain it hadn't already happened.

AT THE MIDNIGHT SONS office, late that afternoon, Charles propped his feet on the corner of Sawyer's desk and twisted the cap off a cold bottle of beer. Across from him, Sawyer leaned forward, resting his elbows on his knees.

"In a few days, I'll be a married man," his brother announced meaningfully.

"Are you having second thoughts?" Charles asked, watching Sawyer closely. If Sawyer *had* had a change of heart, it wasn't too late, but Charles sincerely hoped that wasn't the case.

"Second thoughts? Are you nuts?" Sawyer burst out. "I want to marry Abbey more than I've ever wanted anything in my life. It's just that all at once I realize what a huge responsibility it is to become a husband and a father."

Charles lifted the beer bottle in a silent toast. "Better you than me, little brother."

"I didn't know it was possible to love anyone this much," he said as if he was speaking to himself. "It's almost frightening."

Charles said nothing. Never having been in love himself, he couldn't entirely relate to his brother's feelings. Or could he? He thought of Lanni with her wistful, soul-deep eyes and the way her cheeks flushed a fetching shade of pink when he kissed her. Lanni. She'd felt so soft in his arms. And he remembered how easy and companionable their conversation had been. Charles had always considered himself a somewhat solitary man, self-sufficient and happy in his own company. Now, after meeting Lanni, his life just seemed...lonely. He couldn't help wondering if this was what his brother had experienced when he met Abbey.

Charles didn't know and he wasn't about to ask. Not after the way he'd chided Sawyer for rushing into marriage.

The office door flew open, and John Henderson stepped inside. "Ralph needs to talk to you," he told Sawyer, nodding politely in Charles's direction.

"Problems?"

"Nothing you can't fix," John assured him.

"You go on," Charles said. "I'll finish my beer and get out of your way."

Sawyer disappeared and John was about to leave, as well.

"John," Charles said, stopping him. "I have a question for you."

"Sure." John looked at him expectantly.

"You've met Lanni Caldwell?"

"Sure thing. Duke has, too. He flew her in himself."

Charles rubbed the side of his jaw. Either the beer was more potent that he realized or he was about to stick his foot halfway down his throat. "Is there a reason you and the other pilots haven't...haven't, you know, courted her?"

"We can't see the point," John supplied without a pause. "She's already got her eye on you." Having said that, he walked away, leaving the screen door to slam behind him.

PACKED BOXES were stacked against the living room wall. Lanni groaned and pressed her hands to the small of her back. She'd worked all morning without a break.

A timid knock sounded on the front door. Grateful for the distraction, Lanni opened the door to find Scott and Susan standing on the porch. They both wore forlorn expressions.

"Hiya, kids," Lanni said with a smile.

"Hi," Scott said.

"Do you want to pick wildflowers with us?" Susan asked. Her eyes seemed incredibly large in her small face. "We wanted to get my mom and Sawyer some flowers for the wedding, but "

"But Mom said," Scott picked up the conversation, "we can't go out on the tundra without an adult, and we can't—"

"We can't find an adult to go with us," Susan finished.

"So, you wanna come?" Both children looked up at her hopefully.

"The flowers are real pretty," Susan said.

"We even have a book," Scott told Lanni. He knelt down and removed his backpack. "Mom gave it to us. It's from the library. See?" He handed her the small book, full of color photos and numerous drawings.

"Will you come with us?" Susan asked softly, gazing up at her.

Lanni wasn't sure how anyone had managed to refuse these two. "I haven't had lunch yet," she said, "but I suppose I could make a sandwich and take it with me."

Scott's and Susan's eyes lighted up as if they couldn't believe what they were hearing.

"But I have to be back before five," Lanni said, glancing at her watch. Charles had phoned and asked her to dinner at his house at six. That would give her plenty of time to clean up before meeting him.

"That's okay. We have to be home before that."

The kids followed her into the kitchen, chatting about Scott's dog, Eagle Catcher, while Lanni made herself a cheese-and-tomato sandwich. Since she had the fixings out, she made extras for Scott and Susan, then added cookies and a thermos of juice. Might as well make a regular picnic of it. Almost in afterthought, she packed a can of pepper spray in case they had any trouble with bears.

"I'll change my shoes and be ready in a minute," she said when she'd finished.

"I'll run and tell Mom you're going with us," Scott offered.

Lanni had just laced up her boots when the boy returned. "Mom told me to tell you she appreciates you going with us."

"It'll be fun. We'll learn about wildflowers together, and we'll get a beautiful bouquet of flowers for the wedding." Refrigerated, they should last until then, she thought.

They walked, Lanni in the middle, until Hard Luck was out of sight. The snow-covered peaks of the Brooks Range were visible through the cloud layer to the north. A cool breeze whistled across the tundra, and the flowers bloomed all around them in colorful array.

They found several patches of alpine arnica along their route. The yellow, daisylike flower with its pointed leaves was one of Lanni's favorites.

"We can't get all the same kind," Scott insisted.

"What's the pink flower?" Lanni asked, leafing through the book, which was coded by color. She knelt down beside the plant. "It looks like it might be this one," she said, pointing to the page and picture.

"Parry's wallflower," Susan read slowly.

"It's a member of the mustard family."

"I don't think Mom and Sawyer want a mustard plant at their wedding!" Scott said scornfully.

"But it's pretty," Susan protested. "We don't have to tell them the flower's really some old mustard plant."

"All right, we'll cut some of that, too," Scott agreed, but he didn't sound happy about it.

They walked farther and gathered arctic daisies and calla as well as a handful of northern primroses.

"We aren't supposed to go near the berry bushes," Scott said. He seemed to consider it a silly warning. "I told Mom we wouldn't pick any berries for her wedding, anyway."

"She wasn't worried about that," Lanni explained, relieved that she'd remembered the can of pepper spray. "Brown bears love the berries, and they wouldn't take kindly to sharing with us."

"Bears?" Susan repeated. Her head jerked up and she slowly looked around.

"What's this?" Scott asked, kneeling down on the tundra to point out a deep impression made in the soft, spongy grass.

Lanni squatted down and examined the large footprint. "I think a bear recently crossed here," she said, making sure her voice was calm. "They're probably all over this section of land, especially with so many berries getting ready to ripen."

"A bear was here?" Susan asked.

"Yes, sweetheart, but you don't need to worry. He isn't here now."

"You're sure?"

"No," Lanni said. "But I don't see any bears, do you?"

Both children glanced around.

"Don't worry," Lanni said. "Their natural diet is about eighty percent vegetarian. Brown bears much prefer berries and roots to meat."

"In other words, one could kill us, but he probably wouldn't eat us," Scott suggested.

"I think we have enough wildflowers," Susan said nervously, "don't you?"

"I think so, too," Scott agreed.

"We can go back to Hard Luck if you want," Lanni said, sorry now that she'd mentioned the eating habits of bears. "We can have our picnic on my porch."

"I want to," Susan declared, and Scott nodded eagerly.

Lanni gathered the wildflowers in her arms, and the three of them turned back toward town. She noted that Scott and Susan stayed close to her side.

"What's that?" Scott asked suddenly, his voice cold with fear. He gestured across the tundra.

Lanni had to squint to make out the minuscule brown figure. Her heart thumped wildly. "It...looks like it might be a bear," she whispered.

CHARLES COULDN'T BELIEVE he'd actually invited Lanni to eat a meal he'd cooked himself. Who the hell did he think he was—some gourmet chef? His expertise was limited to a select number of dishes that went into a microwave. He was pretty handy with a camp stove, but he wasn't going to impress Lanni if he poured their dinner out of a pouch.

It was either prepare the meal himself or take her to dinner at the Hard Luck Café. Charles was well aware that he had no culinary skills whatsoever. But serving his own limited fare was better than taking her to Ben's. By morning, the entire population of Hard Luck would have heard about him and Lanni and would delight in speculating about their relationship.

He could see it all now. He wouldn't have a moment's peace with her tonight—or any other night. First Ben would be over to fill their water glasses. Then he'd hang around, sharing the latest gossip the way he always did.

When Ben left, one of the other patrons would pick up the conversation. Before Charles knew it, everyone in the diner would be asking them questions. And they'd all hurry home to spread the word. The situation would be impossible.

More determined than ever to fix dinner himself, Charles scanned his cupboards. He made a pretty decent boxed macaroni and cheese. He could whip that up and serve it with smoked salmon. For dessert there was always canned peaches or dried fruit.

The freezer had several moose steaks left from last winter, but he didn't know how Lanni felt about eating game.

After several minutes Charles slumped down on a kitchen chair. It wasn't any wonder he was a bachelor, he decided. Macaroni and cheese just didn't cut it—not for dinner with company.

He needed help. Tucking his pride in his back pocket, Charles made his way down to the Hard Luck Café. He found Ben writing out the day's menu on a blackboard.

"It's a little early for dinner, isn't it?" Ben asked when he noticed Charles reading over the specials.

"Yeah," he agreed. "Uh, how's the Norwegian pot roast?"

"Damn good, if I do say so myself. I cook it in a Dutch oven with lots of garlic and bacon fat. Then I add a couple of bay leaves and some ginger, and I make the gravy with plenty of sour cream." He pressed his fingertips to his lips and made a loud smacking noise. "You haven't tasted anything better this side of Fairbanks."

Charles grinned. "What do you serve with it?"

"Mashed potatoes, green beans and a jellied salad." Ben eyed him speculatively. "Is there a reason for all these questions?"

"Yeah," Charles said uncomfortably. "I don't suppose you'd consider selling me a couple of those dinners as takeout."

"Takeout? What's the matter, have I got bad breath or something?"

Charles shook his head. "I'm having…a friend over for dinner."

"Who?" Ben cocked his head to one side.

"None of your damn business."

"I could make an intelligent guess. Obviously it's someone you don't want to bring here. Hmm, there's got to be a reason for that."

"Will you or will you not sell me two pot-roast dinners to go?" Charles demanded. Ben was as bad as Sawyer when it came to tramping all over his ego.

"I don't suppose it's Lanni Caldwell?" Ben asked.

"What if it is?"

"Then you got yourself two of the best Norwegian pot-roast dinners you're ever going to taste, and at a bargain price to boot."

Charles pulled his wallet out of his back pocket. "And you've got yourself a deal." He set the cash on the counter. "I'll be back in an hour to pick them up."

"You want a little candlelight and romance to go with that?" Ben teased as he walked out the door.

Charles ignored him.

He was halfway back to the house when he ran into Sawyer.

"Have you seen Scott and Susan?"

"No." Charles wondered at the urgency in his brother's voice.

"What about Lanni?"

"Not since yesterday. Why?"

Sawyer frowned, rubbing his jaw with one hand. "Abbey just told me the three of them went for a walk on the tundra. They were going to cut wildflowers for the wedding bouquet."

"How long have they been gone?"

"Three hours. They were due back an hour ago. Something's wrong. I can feel it in my gut."

Charles stiffened, an unfamiliar fear gnawing at his composure. "Do you know which way they headed?" he asked, trotting toward his truck.

"South, Abbey thinks."

Within minutes the two men were out of Hard Luck, bumping and jolting over the tundra in Charles's truck. Sawyer lifted a pair of binoculars to his eyes and scanned the rolling landscape.

Nothing.

The tundra had already claimed one life in his family. An aunt had disappeared at age five without a trace. Neither man spoke, but Charles knew what Sawyer was thinking, because the same thoughts were crashing through his own mind.

Lanni with those two kids. Talk about the blind leading the blind!

Charles wasn't a man who often prayed. But he did so now, seeking protection for three precious lives.

"There," Sawyer shouted, pointing southwest. "It looks like Lanni's carrying Susan piggyback."

Although Charles couldn't make out the figures yet, he steered in the direction Sawyer indicated. When he saw them, he murmured a silent prayer of thanksgiving.

Lanni and the kids stopped walking as soon as they saw the truck. Susan slid off Lanni's back, and they stood there waiting. The second Charles pulled to a stop Sawyer jumped out, and the children raced toward him.

His brother crouched down and they scrambled into his arms.

"A bear came after us!" Scott cried, his voice trembling. "He was going to have us for dinner, too."

"Lanni saved us," Susan sobbed, circling Sawyer's neck with her arms and squeezing tightly.

Lanni stood no more than two feet away from Charles. For several long, unguarded moments he soaked in the sight of her. Her hair was disheveled, her face red with perspiration and streaked with dirt. Nevertheless he was convinced he'd never seen anyone more beautiful.

"Are you all right?" he asked when he found his voice. His words were taut.

She nodded slowly. "We crossed paths with a bear."

The hair rose on the back of Charles's neck. "Were you hurt?" he asked frantically.

Lanni raised a shaking hand to her mouth. "Oh, God, I was so scared."

Not caring that his brother was watching, Charles hauled her into his arms and hugged her as if he never intended to release her. She came without resistance, buried her face in his chest and wept.

"It's all right," he whispered, stroking her hair. "You're safe now. Nothing's going to happen."

"At first the bear was a long ways away," Scott was saying. "He was just a brown dot."

"We could hardly see him," Susan added.

"Then he started to run straight for us."

"We ran, too," Susan said, "as fast as we could."

"Boy, can those bears run fast," Scott said.

"Then I fell," Susan cried, squeezing Sawyer's neck even tighter.

"I thought she was gonna be dead meat, but Lanni stopped and helped her up. Then Lanni stood on top of a rock and waved her arms and told me and Susan to hide. Lanni shouted like crazy, and when the bear got close she sprayed him with pepper spray. At first it didn't look like it was gonna work. We were afraid the bear was going to get Lanni, but he went away... and then Lanni started to shake real bad."

"The pepper worked," Susan said. "But if it hadn't, Lanni'd be dead, and Scott and me next."

"Oh, Lanni," Charles groaned. Lanni would've sacrificed herself to save the children.

"The bear stood up, too, and he's bigger'n a building!" Scott said.

"He was real, real big," Susan put in.

Sawyer loaded Scott and Susan into the back of the pickup and climbed in after them. The three of them sat there while Charles helped Lanni into the cab, then got in himself.

She pressed her head against his shoulder as if she no longer had the strength to hold it up. "Thank you for coming," she whispered.

Emotion clogged his throat, and it was all he could do to keep from kissing her. To keep from thanking her for being alive.

He gently brushed the hair from her cheek, and she placed her hand over his fingers. The simple touch caused him to shudder with emotion.

"Lanni."

She lifted her head from his shoulder. He didn't know what to say—how to say what was in his heart. Raising her hand to his lips, he planted tender, desperate kisses there.

He struggled for words. "Dear God, Lanni, you could have been killed."

"I know... I know."

Pulling her to him, he blindly searched for her lips. With his kiss he told her what he couldn't communicate in any other way. They kissed with the urgency of two people who recognize how close they've came to losing each other, an urgency mingled with fear. They kissed until the tremors of apprehension were replaced with ones of passion and need.

"I DON'T KNOW why we aren't leaving," Sawyer said to the kids. They were still waiting for Charles to switch on the ignition.

Scott got to his feet and clumped across the bed of the truck to the small window in back of the cab.

"I do," the boy muttered. "Uncle Charles is kissing Lanni."

CHAPTER FOUR

"HAS EVERYONE around here gone crazy?" Charles asked as he walked into the Hard Luck Café two mornings later.

"I imagine you're talking about the wedding," Ben commented, reaching automatically for the coffeepot. He filled a cup for Charles and one for himself.

"Is there anything else?" Charles grumbled under his breath, taking a seat at the counter. He'd never seen anything like it. The entire town was being spruced up for the event. Folks were mowing lawns and cleaning out flower beds. You'd think the president was stopping by for a visit.

The school gymnasium, which was generally used for town meetings and the get-together at Christmas, had never been decorated more elaborately. Even the basketball hoop was filled with silk flowers. He'd like to know what Larry Bird would say if he laid eyes on that!

Since Charles was standing up as best man for his brother, he'd been informed that he'd need to rent a tuxedo. Tuxedos weren't the only wedding paraphernalia that couldn't be obtained in Hard Luck. Sawyer had kept his pilots busy for two entire days making runs to Fairbanks and beyond, collecting everything from tuxes to table napkins. The last he heard, Duke Porter had been sent on a wild-goose chase after a silver punch bowl. Charles wouldn't have believed it if he hadn't heard it with his own ears.

"Are you baking the wedding cake?" he asked Ben.

"Not me," the café proprietor said, raising both hands as if he wouldn't touch that task with a ten-foot pole. "I've got enough on my mind worrying about the rehearsal dinner and the hors d'oeuvres for the reception."

"Tell me," Charles said, shaking his head, "just where does my brother intend to put everyone? Abbey's parents arrive tomorrow, which is fine. Sawyer's putting them up in his house, and he's moving in with me. But there's Abbey's best friend and her husband, plus other family."

Frankly Charles wasn't keen on the idea of sharing his home with his brother, even if it *was* for only one night. Sawyer was an emotional wreck. The closer the wedding grew, the worse Sawyer got. Charles feared his brother would disintegrate into a blithering idiot before noon tomorrow. He wasn't far from it now.

"You think that's bad," Ben said, smiling ironically. "Abbey's got every woman in town rolling these tiny scrolls and tying them with satin ribbons. The hell if I know what she intends to do with them."

"Thank goodness *you're* levelheaded enough not to be gettin' married."

Charles's eyes avoided Ben's. He cleared his throat and glanced over his shoulder to be sure they were alone. "Actually that was something I wanted to talk to you about."

Ben straightened. "Don't tell me you're next? You've gone and fallen in love with Lanni, haven't you?"

"No!" Charles snapped. "Of course not." But then, what did he know about love? If what was happening to Sawyer was any indication, then Charles would have to compare love with a bad case of the flu.

"You're protesting just a bit too loud for me to believe you," Ben said. He walked around the counter and slid onto the stool next to Charles's.

Charles didn't argue. He wished he could find a way to explain away what was happening between him and Lanni. "Have you ever met a woman and known right from that precise moment that— Hell, I don't know how to describe it."

"Like someone kicked you in the gut?"

"Yes," Charles said, grasping at his friend's definition. It was the best way he'd come across to describe what had happened to him the night he'd passed Lanni walking with Duke Porter. It didn't matter that she was with another man. It didn't matter that he and Lanni hadn't said more than a handful of words to each other. It felt as if God had sent a fist straight through the cloudless blue sky to set him straight.

"It happened to me once," Ben said hoarsely, cradling his mug with both hands. He stared into the distance, frowning.

"You know what I'm talking about, then?" Charles prodded.

"I think so," Ben muttered. "But it was a long time ago. Longer than I care to admit." He gazed intently into his coffee, as if that would help him understand the past. "I was a kid, still wet behind the ears. I'd had a little college and kicked around for a while. Then I enlisted and when I finished boot camp, was in San Francisco waiting for my orders to go to Vietnam.

"I met Marilyn at Golden Gate Park. She had long blond hair and was so damned pretty I couldn't take my eyes off her. She was going into her sophomore year in college. We had six weeks together."

"You mean before you were shipped out?" Charles asked.

"Yeah. She didn't want me to go, like I had a choice about it. Marilyn was against the war. But what college kid wasn't? She seemed to believe that if I really loved her, I'd find a way to stay with her. We argued about it. I said some things I regretted later. I'd like to think she regretted what she said to me, too, but I have no way of knowing."

"What happened after you left?"

"Nothing. She was the one in the wrong, I figured. It made me mad she'd be so narrow-minded. What about honor and duty? What about patriotism and commitment? Apparently they meant nothing to her. What kind of man did she think I was to ask me to turn my back on my country? The way I saw it, we had nothing in common."

"So you broke it off."

"Yeah," Ben answered, but he didn't sound happy about it. "She wrote me a couple times, but I never even opened the letters. Just sent them back."

"What about after the war? Did you see her?" If Ben still had strong feelings for her after all these years, surely he must have made some effort to patch things up.

"I was ready to swallow my pride a year later. Once I was stateside, I phoned her. That was when I learned she'd gotten married. According to her mother, she didn't let any grass grow under her feet, either. Four months after I left, she was engaged. I don't mind telling you, it was a shock. We might've only had six weeks together, but they were the best weeks of my life. I loved her then, and even now I've got a soft spot in my heart for her."

Charles didn't know what to say. It seemed to him that Marilyn must not have loved Ben the way he loved her, otherwise she never would have married someone else.

"You know, I really loved her. Thinking about Marilyn was what got me through the craziness in 'Nam. I've got plenty of regrets in this life, but the biggest one is what happened between me and her. I was a fool."

Charles had a few regrets of his own.

"We were both too young, too idealistic in our different ways," Ben continued, "I've paid for that."

Once more Charles felt at a loss as to what to say. He was surprised and saddened by Ben's story. Although he considered Ben a good friend, the older man rarely spoke of his past.

"Are you offering me any advice?" Charles asked.

Ben pondered a moment. "For one thing you gotta trust your feelings."

"My feelings?" He hardly knew what his feelings *were*. As for trusting them . . .

"Yeah. You've met Lanni, and you like her and she likes you. That's great. It doesn't mean you have to leap off the nearest bridge—or into marriage."

Charles thought about Sawyer, and his blood ran cold. Less than a month after meeting Abbey, his brother was taking on a wife and two children. If that didn't constitute a major life change, Charles didn't know what did.

"Tell you the truth, I'm surprised at you," Ben said candidly.

"You mean because I made such a fuss about the way Sawyer and Christian brought women to Hard Luck?"

"No," Ben's voice was thoughtful. "Until now, I'd always kind of figured the two of us were alike. Cast from the same mold, two peas in a pod, that sort of thing."

"How's that?"

"You're a stubborn cuss."

"True." Charles couldn't deny it.

"And a bit of a loner."

Charles nodded.

"I guess what I'm trying to say is, I never expected a woman to affect you this way."

"I don't know what you mean," Charles insisted. All he was doing was sorting through his thoughts.

Ben swallowed the rest of his coffee and slid off the stool. "You asked for my advice, so I'll give it to you. Quit analyzing your feelings to death. Like I said, you gotta trust 'em. You don't need to make any decisions right now. Nothing has to change this minute. Enjoy her."

"I do," Charles mumbled. Too much. That was part of his problem. Soon he'd be back in the field, doing what he loved best. Surveying. He'd always thought of those times alone as necessary. It had always seemed to him that was when his soul caught up with his body. But for the first time, he wasn't looking forward to the solitude he normally craved. He wanted Lanni with him.

Worst of all, when he left for the field this time, Lanni would be right here in Hard Luck with a bunch of love-starved bush pilots eager for her attention. Eager to have him out of the picture. Before long, Bill Landgrin and his pipeline crew would be making excuses to visit town.

Charles gritted his teeth. He didn't want Lanni with any other man. He wanted her with *him*.

"ABBEY!" SAWYER BURST into the library. "I forgot the mints." He announced this as if the world were about to end.

Abbey looked up from the stack of books she was replacing on the shelves and blinked. "The mints?"

"You asked me to have John pick them up this afternoon, but I forgot."

"Oh, the mints. Don't worry about it. You had more than enough on your mind. Just remember to have someone pick up my parents in Fairbanks tomorrow afternoon."

"Tomorrow," he repeated as if making a mental note. "I have the time and place on my schedule at the office. Right?"

"Right." Abbey had given Sawyer the information herself a week earlier. "What about your mother and Robert?" Robert was Sawyer's stepfather.

"She's coming with Christian the morning of the wedding. Oh, I forgot to tell you. Robert won't be with her. With his broken leg, he's finding it too hard to travel. He phoned his regrets."

"I'll meet him later, I guess," Abbey said.

Sawyer slowly lowered himself into a chair. The panicked expression on his face said that keeping track of everyone's comings and goings had become more than he could manage. "I've never looked forward to getting something over with this much."

Abbey shrugged. "You're the one who insisted on putting together a wedding in two weeks' time!"

"Don't remind me. I have no one to blame for this but myself."

Abbey was about to put an encyclopedia back on the shelf when Sawyer reached out and grabbed her around the waist.

She let out a small cry of surprise as he pulled her onto his lap. His arms brought her close.

"Why didn't you just suggest we elope and be done with it?" he chided. "I've never gone through this before, and like a fool, I thought organizing a wedding was no big deal. In case you haven't noticed, woman, I'm a wreck."

"I've noticed," she said seriously, resting her hands on his shoulders, "but I agreed with you that a formal wedding was a good idea." She paused. "For me, for my children and parents, it's a symbol of our love. Our marriage. It also marks the beginning of our new life. I happen to think symbols and ceremonies are important." She dropped a kiss on his forehead. "I love you all the more for insisting on it."

"I swear I'm going crazy."

"It'll all be over in two short days," she reminded him.

"I wish it was over now."

"Patience, my love."

He stroked her cheek with his callused palm. "I had no idea waiting to make love to you would be this difficult," he said in a husky murmur.

The gentleness of his touch and the agony in his words pierced Abbey's heart. She closed her eyes and buried her face in his shoulder. It was at her request that they had decided to wait until their wedding night. And it moved her deeply that Sawyer had agreed. She was convinced no one had ever loved her this much. Emotion filled her chest, making it difficult to breathe.

"I love you, Sawyer O'Halloran."

"It's a damn good thing you do, because I'd hate to think I was putting on a cummerbund for nothing."

Abbey giggled and kissed him with a thoroughness that left them both dizzy.

"I have the feeling," Sawyer said, pausing to clear his throat, "you're going to be well worth the wait."

LANNI VOLUNTEERED to answer the phones for Sawyer when Abbey's parents arrived early Friday afternoon. Sawyer introduced her to Wayne and Marie Murray, and Lanni liked the middle-aged couple immediately.

"Entertain your guests," she urged Sawyer, "and don't worry about anything here. I can take care of the phones."

"You're sure you don't mind?" He looked apprehensive, as if he might be imposing. "You've been helping out almost every day this week."

"I'm positive. In fact I appreciate the break. I spent the morning cleaning out my grandmother's place, and it's tedious work."

Sawyer hesitated, glancing over his shoulder to be sure he wasn't keeping his future in-laws waiting. Scott and Susan were busy introducing them around.

"Speaking of your grandmother," he began, "I don't suppose you've mentioned her to Charles, have you?"

"No." The answer was clipped. She avoided his gaze.

"I just wondered . . ."

"I thought you might have told him."

"No, I figured you'd want to do it."

She hadn't told Charles because she feared what would happen once he learned she was related to Catherine Fletcher. And the longer she avoided the issue, the more difficult it was to tell him. She almost wished that Sawyer *had* said something.

"You'll tell him?" Sawyer asked.

She nodded.

"When?"

"Soon," she promised. After the wedding, when life in Hard Luck had returned to normal. She hadn't purposely deceived him. Not any more than Sawyer had, or anyone else who knew her reason for being in Hard Luck.

"Good," the groom-to-be said decisively, then disappeared out the door.

Sawyer's desk was in a general state of chaos. She was doing her best to straighten his papers, schedules and messages when the office door opened and Charles stepped inside. He stopped abruptly the instant he saw her.

Lanni's heartbeat thundered in her ears at the sight of him.

Their eyes met and held.

"Hello again," she said. She knew instinctively that Charles was uncomfortable with the strength of their attraction. She didn't need anyone to tell her he was fighting this feeling, either. She recognized that because she was fighting it herself.

"Hi," he said a little awkwardly. "Uh, where's Sawyer?"

"He's out of the office for a while," she explained. "Abbey's parents just arrived."

"That's right; I'd forgotten." But he still didn't leave. "I came to ask about the wedding rehearsal this evening."

Lanni walked over to Sawyer's desk and flipped the pages of his appointment calendar. "Says here it's supposed to start at seven."

"I know that much. I was just wondering how formal I'm supposed to dress for this."

"Nothing fancy. What you have on now is fine."

"Great." Charles moved farther into the office. "Were you planning on attending the wedding tomorrow?"

"Yes. I'm looking forward to it." Although she hadn't received a formal invitation, both Sawyer and Abbey had asked her to come. "I'll be playing the piano for the rehearsal later, too."

"You will?"

"The man bringing the recorded music won't be available until the wedding itself. He's coming from Fairbanks."

"I see. Speaking of the wedding," Charles said, "I was wondering if you'd... consider attending it with me—" he paused as if the words had stuck in his throat "—as my date?"

Lanni smiled softly. You'd almost think he dreaded her response. "I'd like that very much."

"Great," he said, grinning broadly. "Shall we meet at the church? I'd offer to stop by the house and personally escort you, but unfortunately I'm going to have my hands full with Sawyer."

"He told me you're going to be his best man."

"I just hope he lasts through the ceremony. I've never met a more nervous groom."

"He'll be fine."

"Yeah, I'm sure he will."

Lanni's fingers fumbled with the papers on Sawyer's desk.

"Will you be going over to Ben's for the dinner tonight after the rehearsal?" Charles asked.

She nodded. From what she'd heard, at least half the town would be on hand for the after-rehearsal dinner.

"I'll look for you there." Charles seemed to brighten.

"I'll probably be a little late, though," Lanni said, regretting now that she'd volunteered to be part of the crew that would decorate the church. "I promised I'd help get the sanctuary ready for the wedding."

"I'll save a seat for you," Sawyer promised, "next to me."

Lanni liked the idea of that and smiled.

"I'll see you at seven, then," he said, backing out of the trailer.

She raised her hand in farewell. "Until seven."

Feeling oddly shaky after the short encounter, Lanni pulled out a chair and sat down. It wasn't the first time she'd observed that being around Charles left her feeling distinctly weak in the knees.

CHARLES WAS HAVING one hell of a time paying attention. This was supposed to be a practice before the actual wedding. A rehearsal, so everyone would know when to sit and stand. So Charles would know when to steer his lovesick brother toward the altar, when to jab him in the ribs signaling it was time to repeat his vows.

He *should* be paying attention. Instead, his gaze repeatedly wandered over to Lanni, who sat behind the old upright piano.

Again and again his eyes were drawn to her lips. Why he should choose that precise moment to remember how soft and sweet her mouth was, he'd never know.

Thank heaven no one could read his mind. He'd probably be arrested for harboring such sensual thoughts in a house of God. If the evening was starting out like this—with him so distracted he couldn't see straight—Charles hated to think about the dinner later.

It was bad enough that—

"Charles," Reverend Wilson, the circuit minister, cut into his musings, "were you listening?"

"Sorry," he muttered, pulling his eyes and thoughts away from Lanni.

"Pay attention," Sawyer grumbled. "I'm going to need you."

As if Charles hadn't figured that one out. What he hadn't figured out, though, was where all these people had come from, and more important, where they were going to sleep. Thank goodness his mother and Christian weren't arriving until the morning, especially since Sawyer had given Christian's bed to Abbey's matron of honor and her husband.

Reverend Wilson stood in front of the group. "I think we'd best run through this one more time. I sense some . . . confusion here, and we want the actual ceremony to go as smoothly as possible."

Charles groaned inwardly.

"All right, let's start from the beginning."

It took the better part of an hour to go through the ceremony one last time. Charles did his damnedest to pay attention, although it remained a struggle to keep his eyes off Lanni. She looked so damn beautiful in her white cotton dress that he wondered how anyone could *not* stare at her.

When Reverend Wilson finally dismissed them, Charles casually made his way over to the piano. Almost everyone else had vacated the church in a rush— as if fearful that the good pastor might find some excuse to call them back.

As Charles approached the piano, Lanni was straightening a stack of sheet music.

"You did a great job," he told her, but in actual fact he couldn't have identified a single piece she'd played.

"Thank you."

"If you want, I'll wait for you and we can walk over to Ben's together," he suggested.

Lanni looked at Pearl Inman, who stood at the back of the church holding a bag of huge white ribbons. "You'd better go on without me," she said with reluctance. "It'll take ten or fifteen minutes to put up the pew bows, and everyone will wonder where you are if you don't show up right away."

"Okay," he agreed readily enough, although he would have preferred to stay. Unfortunately his duties as best man were interfering with his plans to spend time with her.

When Charles arrived at the Hard Luck Café most of the others were there. He barely recognized the place. Ben had set up six-foot-long tables and covered them with white linen cloths. Each table was adorned with a decorative paper wedding bell and a smattering of brightly colored confetti.

Charles went straight to the head table to greet Abbey and Sawyer and the other members of the wedding party. "We need an extra chair here," he said, edging his way past the adjoining table to grab one before anyone else could claim it.

"An extra chair?" Sawyer asked, "Who for?"

"Lanni," Charles answered, glaring at his brother, daring him to make an issue of it. He shoved the chair viciously into place beside his.

"Lanni, of course," Sawyer said, sliding Charles another of his know-it-all looks. His brother leaned over and whispered something to Abbey, who glanced in Charles's direction and grinned.

Charles resisted the urge to remind his brother and Abbey that it was impolite to whisper.

Instead, he took his seat. Tantalizing smells wafted from the kitchen. Ben stepped into the crowded room, wearing a chef's hat and a fresh white apron.

"Dinner is served," he said with uncharacteristic formality. Then he instructed everyone to take their plates to the buffet table.

Rather than stand in line, Charles decided to wait until Lanni could join him. As she'd promised, it didn't take long. The side door opened and she walked in.

Because of the noise, he raised his hand to attract her attention, rather than call out to her. With any luck she'd see he was seated at the head table.

However, before she saw Charles, Ted Richards, one of Sawyer's new pilots, waylaid her. It was obvious that the man had asked Lanni to join him at his table.

Charles held his breath, wondering what she'd do. Even from this distance, he could see how persuasive the pilot was. With a sweeping gesture, Ted held out a chair for Lanni as if to say that her sitting next to him would be the greatest honor of his life.

Charles's hands tightened.

"It looks to me like Ted's about to steal your girl," someone whispered from behind him. So intent was Charles on what was happening between Lanni and the pilot, he didn't know who'd spoken.

"Excuse me," he said, impatiently making his way around several other people.

"Lanni," he said, interrupting Ted. "I've got a seat for you up front."

"I asked her to sit with me," Ted pointed out.

"I asked her first."

"Charles did ask me earlier this afternoon," Lanni explained in what Charles thought was a much too apologetic tone.

"What is it with those O'Halloran men?" Ted loudly asked a pilot sitting nearby. "Bringing women into Hard Luck was to keep us pilots happy. It was the main reason I took the job! We don't get so much as a chance with them, though, do we? The minute a decent woman arrives, one of the O'Hallorans takes her for himself."

Charles would have asked the hotheaded pilot to apologize if Lanni hadn't quickly announced, "I'm starved."

"Ben outdid himself," Charles said, steering her toward the buffet line. "He ordered honey baked ham from Anchorage and cooked up his own scalloped potatoes. It looks like there might be a salad or two up there, as well. And I heard a rumor that there's blueberry cobbler for dessert."

"It all sounds wonderful. I'm so hungry I could eat a moose."

"Sorry, that's not on the menu until next week," he teased.

The meal proved as delicious as Charles had expected. Afterward, there were a few short humorous speeches. Charles made one himself, about his brother being a man who knew what he wanted and knew how to get it.

Together Abbey and Sawyer stood, their arms around each other's waists. They took turns thanking all those who had contributed to making their wedding day possible. Scott and Susan sat with their grandparents, beaming.

Hardly aware of what he was doing, Charles reached for Lanni's hand under the table and gripped it. "I'll walk you home," he whispered in her ear.

"What about the bachelor party?" Lanni asked. "Doesn't that start now?"

"So I'll be a few minutes late. It's no big deal."

"You're sure?"

He nodded. He hoped Lanni was as eager to be alone with him as he was with her. No doubt their leaving together would be cause for speculation, but it didn't worry him. Not at all.

He made his farewells and promised to return quickly.

They walked hand in hand toward Catherine Fletcher's old house. Charles tried not to think about Lanni living there. It bothered him, yet he knew his reaction should be gratitude that she had a decent place to stay. The only other alternative was one of those worthless cabins, and Charles certainly didn't want her there.

"You should have stuck around for the party," Lanni said, a smile in her voice. "You know what they're going to say, don't you?"

"No." He did of course, but he really didn't care.

Her smile was sassy and provocative as she turned, walking backward in front of him, hands clasped behind her. "I heard Pearl Inman say there's going to be another wedding in Hard Luck soon," she said in a low, sultry voice. "If I were you, I'd be running for cover."

Charles swallowed tightly. Another wedding. He and Lanni? He tensed, then remembered Ben's advice. *Nothing has to change this minute.* "Let folks talk if that's what makes them happy."

"Fortunately for you I don't think Pearl was referring to us."

Charles frowned. "Then just who was she talking about?"

Lanni blinked. "You mean you don't know?"

"No."

"Dotty Harlow and Pete Livengood."

"Dotty? You mean the nurse who's going to take over at the health clinic?" He watched as the breeze flirted with Lanni's long hair. Its magical fingers stirred up the softness, and once more his gaze was drawn to her enticing, kissable lips.

"Dotty and Pete have been quite an item of late," Lanni informed him.

"You're so damned beautiful." The words slipped out before he could censor them.

She lowered her eyes and blushed.

Embarrassed that he'd let the remark slip, Charles opened the small gate outside the house and walked her to the front porch. With all the men in town gathering for Sawyer's bachelor party, he didn't need to worry about Ted or John or any of the others making time with her.

"Thank you for walking me home," Lanni said, standing on the first step.

"Thank *you* for allowing me to do it." The proper little speech made him feel a bit old-fashioned—"gentlemanly" his mother would have said—but it felt . . . right.

Neither of them spoke, then both, at precisely the same moment, moved together.

Lanni wrapped her arms around his neck as he slipped his around her waist. Their kiss was sweet, then grew passionate. It was better than he'd imagined, better than he'd remembered.

His hands ached to feel her breasts, and she sighed as if reading his thoughts. Gently he cupped one breast and swirled his thumb across the hardened nipple, almost lightheaded with the quick response. Lanni threaded her fingers though his hair as their tongues continued to duel.

All at once they broke apart, as if they were afraid to continue. As if they were afraid of where it would lead them.

Trembling, she lifted a hand to her face and brushed the hair from her cheek. After a moment she suggested. "It might...be a good idea if you joined your friends."

Charles didn't want to leave. Not now. But he knew she was right, knew he had no other choice. Still, the temptation to stay was almost more than he could resist.

"There's a dance following the wedding," he said.

"Yes, I know."

His eyes bore into hers. "I'm not very good on my feet."

She said nothing.

"Save the first dance for me, all right?"

Lanni broke into a smile and nodded.

Charles turned away and hurried back to Ben's. He winced as he realized he'd actually asked her to save a dance for him. Well, he supposed a man didn't voluntarily make a fool of himself without a damn good reason. A sentimental fool, yet. True, he didn't want anyone else dancing with her, but it was more than that.

He was looking for an excuse to hold her. An excuse to wrap his arms around her.

Intuitively Charles knew that whatever he felt for Lanni was an emotion he shouldn't label.

CHAPTER FIVE

CHARLES GAZED UP at the bright blue sky. The Baron twin-engine aircraft with its Midnight Sons logo descended toward the field at Hard Luck. The last time he'd seen his mother had been six months ago. He didn't think of himself as a good son. Since their father's death, Christian and Sawyer had made more of an effort to keep in touch with her.

Ellen was content, and for that Charles was grateful. She deserved a bit of happiness after the hardship of the past forty years. First the war in Europe, which had wiped out her family, then the years spent in a miserable marriage to his father.

The plane touched down smoothly and taxied to a standstill. Charles opened the door. Christian descended first, then turned back to offer his mother a helping hand. Duke Porter, the pilot, climbed out next, and with a respectful wave, left them alone.

Ellen stood and held her small hat in place with one hand as she surveyed the field, and the town just beyond. It took her a moment to realize Charles was waiting for her. A smile touched her lips as she hurried down the steps.

She looked petite and fragile in her pale blue suit. She was a beautiful woman, graceful and exquisitely boned, and as out of place in this harsh land as a hothouse orchid. Charles had never understood what had possessed his father to marry such a delicate woman, knowing where he would be bringing her to live.

"Charles," Ellen cried, hugging him. "Oh, my, don't you look handsome!"

Charles edged his index finger between his neck and the confining collar of his starched white dress shirt. He'd be lucky if the damned thing didn't strangle him before the end of the day.

"You in a tuxedo!" Christian exclaimed. "I don't believe it."

"Believe it," Charles said with a cocky grin. "Sawyer rented one for you, too. It's at the house waiting for you as we speak."

The laughter drained out of Christian's eyes. "You're joking."

"Do I look like I'm making this up?" Charles asked. "You'd better hurry. Sawyer's on pins and needles as it is. It's your turn to keep him occupied while I take Mother over to meet Abbey."

Christian muttered something Charles couldn't hear, but from his tone, that was probably just as well. "It's good to see you, too, big brother."

Charles chuckled and offered Ellen his arm. "You're going to like Abbey," he told her.

"I'm crazy about her already," she said, and slipped her gloved hand into the crook of his arm. "She's managed something I thought was impossible."

"What's that?"

Ellen eyes filled with surprise, as if to say Charles should know very well what she was talking about. "She convinced one of my sons to take a wife. You have no idea how long I've been waiting for one of you to come to your senses. Not only that, she's made me an instant grandmother. I could kiss her feet."

Charles was astonished. "You *want* to be a grand-mother?"

"What woman my age doesn't?" Ellen asked. "I waited long enough to have children, but I swear I've been far more impatient for grandchildren. I can't tell you how grateful I am that Robert's daughter had the good sense to marry young."

"Scott and Susan are going to love you."

"As well they should," Ellen said, and laughed softly. "I plan to spoil them rotten."

Charles was still reeling from his mother's revelation.

"Now let me take a look at you," she said. She stepped back and studied Charles, then raised her hand to her lips. "Oh, Charles, you look dashing." She brushed her white glove across the top of his shoulder. "You make me proud, son."

Charles wasn't accustomed to dealing with praise, especially from his mother. "Uh, thank you."

Ellen's smile wavered as she moved into place beside him and squared her shoulders. "Now take me to meet my daughter-in-law-to-be before I make a fool of my-self by breaking into tears." She snapped open her handbag and withdrew a lace-edged handkerchief, which she pressed to the corner of each eye.

"Aw, Mom," Charles said, guiding her toward the pickup. "Don't tell me you're going to cry at Sawyer's wedding."

"Of course I am," she said. "It's my right and I've earned it."

HARDLY A SINGLE SEAT remained empty in the small community church. Lanni felt fortunate to find a place to sit. An air of festivity filled the room, as though each person present was in some way responsible for Sawyer's marrying Abbey Sutherland.

A hush fell over the gathering when Charles and Sawyer appeared and walked toward the altar. They turned slightly to await the approach of Abbey and her attendants.

Because the church didn't have a pipe organ, the couple had opted for taped music and an elaborate sound system. The first notes of the wedding march soared through the small church. Everyone stood and turned toward the center aisle as Abbey entered on her father's arm.

She wore a pale peach, floor-length dress, her hair wreathed in a garland of apple blossoms. She carried a bouquet of white roses mingled with yellow and lavender wildflowers.

They were similar to the ones Lanni had picked with the children the fateful day they'd encountered the bear. Those flowers had gotten lost in the trauma that followed. But apparently Abbey had seen to it that a few of the delicate tundra blossoms were added to her bouquet.

Lanni had seen many a bride in her time and had participated in more weddings than she cared to count. Every bride was beautiful. Every wedding was special. But the happiness shining in Abbey's face as she looked toward the front of the church where Sawyer stood waiting brought unexpected tears to Lanni's eyes. The love that flowed between them was visible to all.

Lanni wasn't the only one affected. Across the aisle from her stood Ben Hamilton. She nearly didn't recognize him without his apron. He reached into his back pocket and took out a crumpled handkerchief and loudly blew his nose. He glanced around self-consciously, then rubbed his fist across his eyes.

Ben weeping! She was astounded by that for some reason. But since her own eyes were blurry with tears of joy, Lanni couldn't very well blame anyone else for reacting the same way.

At that moment Abbey and Sawyer joined hands and stepped in front of Reverend Wilson. Susan and Scott stood beside them. Susan's dress was made from the same material as Abbey's, and her hair was adorned by a garland. Scott stood next to Sawyer in a miniature tuxedo and cummerbund.

When her eyes had cleared, Lanni turned her attention to Charles. She experienced a twinge of pride at what a distinguished-looking man he was. Watching Charles reminded her that time was fast running out.

Soon she wouldn't have an excuse to remain in Hard Luck. Her family was already full of questions. But she couldn't very well admit that she strongly suspected she was falling in love with Charles O'Halloran!

Abbey handed her bridal bouquet to her matron of honor and joined hands with Sawyer. Reverend Wilson asked her to repeat her vows. Her voice didn't hesitate, didn't waver. She seemed to be saying she'd never been more confident of any action she'd ever taken.

"I solemnly swear to love . . ."

LOVE. CHARLES HEARD Abbey speak, and the word leapt into his mind's eye as if it had been boldly printed. All this time he hadn't understood why Sawyer found it so necessary to rush Abbey to the altar. He didn't understand why his brother was in such an all-fired hurry to tie the knot. He'd already waited thirty-three years to marry—what was another three or four months?

To Charles's way of thinking, the least Sawyer could have done was give Abbey time to get settled in Hard Luck. The move from Seattle was a major transition for her and the children. One life change was enough, without adding a marriage with all its adjustments to the equation.

But right now, at this moment, Charles recognized the depth of emotion that bound Sawyer and Abbey. They were very much in love. Waiting a month, three months, a year, would change nothing. Their commitment was as strong now as it would be in twenty years' time.

One look at the two of them standing before God, family and friends was all Charles needed to convince him of that truth. Funny he hadn't recognized it sooner. Funny how blind he'd been to what had been obvious to everyone else.

Love. He risked a look in Lanni's direction. Breathless emotion clenched at his chest as their eyes met. He could see the bright tears that sparkled in hers as she offered him a soft smile.

"... *honor,*" Abbey continued.

HONOR. LANNI TORE her gaze away from Charles. Her heart pounded so fast and loud she grew dizzy. Abbey, Sawyer, the children and Reverend Wilson slowly faded from her view as she focused her attention solely on Charles. Although they'd been together only hours earlier, she felt almost desperate for the sight of him.

She loved this man. Loved him. Briefly she closed her eyes while her mind acknowledged the truth. She wasn't falling in love. She *was* in love.

It wasn't possible, the logical side of her argued. They hadn't known each other long enough. He was older. A loner. *An O'Halloran.* She couldn't love him. Not without creating all kinds of problems for both of them.

Lanni opened her eyes and lifted her head. Once again her gaze slid deeply into his. What she saw there was enough to convince her that nothing was worth more than having this man in her life. She could live another hundred years, and she'd never find anyone she'd love as much.

Had they not been in a church, in the midst of a wedding ceremony, she would have pushed her way into the aisle and run to his side.

Abbey finished repeating her vows and Sawyer began his. *"Before God, I hereby solemnly vow to cherish..."*

CHERISH. HE'D TALK to Lanni, Charles decided. Reason all this out. Together, they'd make some sense of their feelings. Plan for the future. He wouldn't rush her, wouldn't pressure her. It had taken him thirty-five years to find a woman like Lanni, but now that he had, he was willing to do whatever was necessary to keep her in his life.

"I DO," ABBEY SAID, her voice ringing clearly through the church.

"I do, too," Scott added.

"Me, too," Susan chimed in, not wanting to be left out.

The congregation laughed, and Lanni noted there was more than one wet eye in the crowd. Reverend Wilson made his final statement, and then Sawyer O'Halloran kissed his wife.

A spontaneous burst of applause broke out. Ben reached for his kerchief a second time. He blew his nose, and the sound, very much like the honk of a goose, echoed against the church walls.

Scott and Susan led the procession out of the church. The townspeople of Hard Luck spilled out after them.

Somehow in the crush Charles found Lanni. His hand reached for hers and he drew her aside. She knew he was needed at the reception; she was, too. Abbey had asked her to cut the cake.

Neither moved. Or spoke.

Did she dare hope he'd felt the same magic she had during the wedding service? Did she dare believe Charles loved her? Her heart refused to beat. Her lungs forgot to breathe.

People stepped around them, laughing, talking, joking.

Slowly, because she desperately needed to touch him, she raised her hand. Her palm settled against his cheek. He was warm and solid and wonderful.

Wordlessly he drew her into his arms.

"Lanni—"

"I know. I know."

"You felt it, too?"

She nodded.

Charles struggled for words, then shrugged helplessly. "I can't talk now."

She nodded, understanding.

"Later. All right?" Releasing her, he moved away, then—as if he couldn't bear to leave her—turned back. Holding her face between his hands, he kissed her, using his lips, his tongue, his teeth, to tell her what he felt. He took a deep, calming breath before he hurried toward the school gymnasium, where the reception was being held.

It took Lanni a minute to compose herself. She felt like laughing and weeping at the same time. How she'd ever explain this to her family she didn't know. Didn't *want* to know. They'd tell her she'd lost her senses. It was only natural, they'd tell her, to feel this kind of joy in the middle of a wedding service.

They wanted her to fall in love, but not with Charles O'Halloran.

She wouldn't wait to tell them, she decided. For the first time in her life she was truly in love. If no one else, Matt, her brother, would understand. Karen, her former sister-in-law, would, too. And if she was lucky, so would her parents. But before she told them she needed to tell Charles that Catherine Fletcher was her grandmother.

HE WAS POSSIBLY the worst best man Sawyer could have chosen, Charles thought later. He was part of the reception line, but he couldn't concentrate on greeting friends and family. He suspected he hadn't spoken a single sensible word from the moment he took his place next to his mother.

"Charles," Ellen whispered when the crowd began to thin. "What's wrong with you?"

"Wrong?"

"Who is it you keep craning your neck to see?"

Charles wasn't sure she was ready for this. "I met someone very special, Mother. As soon as we're finished here, I'd like to introduce you."

Ellen's jaw slackened, and she laid a hand on his forearm. "Charles, are you telling me— Are you saying you've fallen in love?"

This time he didn't hesitate. "Yes."

"Oh, my heavens!" Ellen placed her free hand over her heart. "When? Who is she? Why didn't you say something sooner?"

Charles grinned. "Actually Lanni and I haven't known each other long."

"That certainly didn't stop Sawyer."

He laughed outright. "So I noticed."

"I don't care what anyone might say, the minute I met Abbey I realized she was the perfect choice for him."

Charles eyed his mother skeptically. "You'd say that if Sawyer announced he was marrying a gorilla. The fact that Abbey comes complete with grandchildren must elevate her to the level of sainthood."

"Don't you pooh-pooh me, young man," Ellen said, tapping his arm in reproach. "It's true I'm overjoyed that at least one of my sons is getting married. But I want it understood right now that I couldn't be happier with Sawyer's choice."

"Yes, Mother," Charles replied with mock timidity.

Ellen glared up at him. "Now stop. Tell me about your young lady."

"She isn't mine. Not yet," he amended. "Lanni's another one of the women Christian hired. She's working for Midnight Sons as a secretary. She's from Seattle, at least I think so. That's where she's been living for the past four years, anyway. She recently graduated from the University of Washington."

"Point her out to me," Ellen urged.

Charles directed her attention across the room to the table where Lanni was busy cutting and serving slices of wedding cake. He couldn't look at her and not be stirred in some way. He observed with pleasure how friendly and open she was, taking time to chat with each person in line. He found it difficult to pull his gaze back to his mother.

"The blonde?" Ellen asked.

"Yes."

"Oh, Charles, she's lovely."

"She's the most beautiful person I ever met."

Ellen gently patted his arm. "What a sweet thing to say."

Charles still couldn't force his eyes away from Lanni. "She's too young for me."

"Fiddlesticks. You're what—six, seven years older?"

"Ten."

"Does the age difference bother her?"

He had to think about that. "She's never said."

"Then I doubt she cares."

"I'm often gone weeks on end." He tried another argument. "I have to be—it's my job."

"Does she object?"

"I don't know. We've never discussed it."

"Ask her," Ellen advised with perfect logic.

He paused, marveling at her easy acceptance of Lanni—and of her son's feelings for a woman who was a virtual stranger. "I want you to get to know her, Mother."

"I'll look forward to that."

Abbey and Sawyer broke away from the reception line. The disc jockey who'd been hired to play music for the wedding dance had set up his equipment, and the first strains of a haunting melody filled the gymnasium.

Sawyer drew Abbey into his arms and danced with his bride. Studying his brother, Charles noticed that he moved with grace and a surprisingly relaxed air.

He heard Ellen's voice and turned back to her. "I want you to be happy," she was saying. "I mean that, Charles. I'd be delighted to see you find happiness with that lovely girl. I am really looking forward to a houseful of grandchildren."

The way he was feeling at the moment, Charles would have enjoyed getting started on the project just as soon as it could be arranged.

He settled his mother in a comfortable chair. Pearl Inman joined Ellen, and the two women hugged.

"If you'll excuse me," Charles said, eager to hurry over to Lanni.

"Of course." Ellen seemed just as anxious to dismiss him.

He was halfway across the room when he turned back to discover Ellen and Pearl with their heads close together, their mouths going a mile a minute. Charles considered the elderly nurse his mother's only real friend in Hard Luck.

His mother had never adjusted to life in Alaska. Charles was convinced, perhaps unfairly, that she'd never tried hard enough. True, there'd been a brief period when she might have found happiness in Hard Luck and in her marriage—but Catherine Fletcher's bitterness had destroyed that, and in the process whatever joy his parents had achieved.

Charles didn't wish Catherine ill, but he was thankful she no longer lived in town. It would be just like her to try to ruin this day for his mother.

Lanni smiled when he approached her. "Are you ready for some cake?"

"Sure, but how about a dance first?"

Lanni glanced at Louise Gold, one of the townspeople and a particular friend of Abbey's. "Go on," Louise urged. "Most everyone had cake."

Charles thanked her. He noted that nine-year-old Ronny was attempting to help his mother—if help was the word—by scooping up any discarded frosting with the tip of his index finger and sneaking it inside his suit pocket. Little Chrissie Harris and her dad, Mitch, stood nearby, watching him with amusement and enjoying their generous slices of cake.

"I've been looking forward to dancing with you," Lanni told Charles, and offered him her hand.

"Just remember I'm not much good at this," he reminded her. They stepped onto the makeshift dance floor. Charles was willing to agree to just about anything for an excuse to hold her. Even if it meant acting like a fool in front of the whole town.

Fortunately the disc jockey had chosen to play a slow number. Charles gathered Lanni in his arms and nearly sighed aloud when she slipped her arms around him. He didn't do much more than shuffle back and forth. At least he wasn't stepping on her feet.

Lanni tucked her head against his shoulder, and he closed his eyes. His chest ached with what he felt for her. He wanted to ask her about what had happened between them in the church during Abbey and Sawyer's wedding. But he couldn't bear to release her, so the question would have to wait.

The song ended, and Charles made a pretense of breaking away. Before the next song started, he already had her in his arms.

Unfortunately the disc jockey started playing one of the fast-paced songs from the seventies. High-pitched male voices chanted something about staying alive.

Couples jerked their bodies in every which direction. Charles figured if he and Lanni were going to survive the song, it wouldn't be on the dance floor.

He scanned the room, then reached for her hand and drew her away. There was absolutely no chance of finding a quiet corner in which to talk. So Charles led her out of the building and into the bright sunlight.

"You want us to dance out here?" Lanni teased.

"Not dance," he said, bringing her back into the circle of his arms. The distance between their mouths felt like the most urgent journey he'd ever made. Charles didn't stop to consider what he was doing. He realized in some vague way that anyone walking outside would stumble upon them. He didn't care.

Lanni moaned and responded with the same pent-up desperation that had driven him. He was greedy for her, needed to put into action everything he was feeling. She tasted so good, so damn good. Their tongues met in a loving duel. And her softness, the smoothness of her skin, the glitter of her satiny hair in the sunlight, made him want to hold her, touch her, forever.

"I couldn't wait a second longer," he said in a husky whisper.

"I couldn't, either."

His chest heaved, and he waited until he'd had a chance to catch his breath. Glancing quickly around, he steered her toward the playground.

"Where are we going?" Lanni asked.

"To the swings."

She pressed her head to his shoulder. "I've always loved the swings. When I was a little girl I'd pump and pump and aim for the sky."

Charles set her in the U-shaped seat and stood in front of her. He grasped the heavy chains. "I think the

Fates must have an excellent sense of humor,'' he said as he drew the swing forward.

"Why's that?"

He released the chains and stepped back as Lanni swayed gently back and forth.

"I gave Sawyer such a hard time about falling in love with Abbey. I was so sure something like this couldn't happen, let alone practically overnight."

For a breathless moment, Lanni said nothing. "You believe differently now?"

"Yes. I *know* differently. Sawyer nearly lost Abbey because of me."

Her eyes widened with surprise.

"I was worried about what had happened to my levelheaded brother. Like I told you, I just didn't believe it was possible to feel the way he did. So in my own stupid way I tried to fix things by offering Abbey and the kids their airfare home. I figured out of sight, out of mind."

"But Abbey didn't leave."

"No, thank heaven. She stayed. And now you're here, and I think I'd shoot the man who tried to convince you to go."

She looked away from him. "Charles, I need to—"

"No," he interrupted, "let me finish. I have to say this. From the moment we met, I felt a connection with you. Later, when you were walking home with Duke Porter— Even now I can't find the words to describe what happened."

"In church this afternoon."

"Yes, again, only much stronger."

"I felt it, too, Charles." Her voice was faint.

"I know nothing about love, Lanni. All I know is what I feel for you. I'm not comfortable with it. The fact is, I'm not sure what to do about it."

"Are you trying to say you love me?" she asked.

"Yes," he answered starkly.

"Oh, Charles."

He wasn't sure what he'd expected, but not this woebegone look that crowded her features together as if she was in pain.

"I realize this is a hell of a thing to throw at you now," he said hurriedly, "but I had this feeling that I *had* to tell you or it was going to burn a hole straight through me."

"I... love you, too."

His shoulders relaxed. At least he wasn't in this predicament alone. "Well, where do we go from here?"

"Do we have to go anywhere?" she asked.

"I guess not." He was almost ashamed to hear the relief in his voice. But the idea of going where Sawyer had gone, terrified Charles. He wasn't ready for marriage. His feelings were too new. He needed time to adjust to the fact that he was in love before complicating his life with an irrevocable commitment. Because if he ever *did* get married, it had to be forever.

He pulled the swing toward him and gave her a loving kiss. "We should get back to the reception."

"I know." She didn't sound eager to return.

"My mother's dying to meet you."

"I want to meet her, too."

Hand in hand, they entered the gymnasium. Several couples were dancing, but because of the shortage of women, Ben Hamilton and John Henderson were waltzing around the room alone, without partners. Duke Porter eyed Lanni—and Charles—as if to gauge how likely she'd be to accept a dance with him. Every other unattached man seemed to be gazing at her just as avidly.

The last person Charles expected to have to give her up to, though, was his own younger brother.

"Hello, beautiful," Christian said, planting himself in front of Lanni.

"Hello, yourself," Charles answered.

"I wasn't talking to you."

"Hello," Lanni responded.

"Can I have this dance and the next one and the one after that?" Christian asked.

Uncertain, Lanni looked at Charles. "Perhaps later," she said kindly. "I promised Charles I'd meet his mother."

"Great," Christian announced. "I'll tag along, and if I'm lucky my big bad brother might find it in his heart to introduce you to me, as well."

Charles didn't know what kind of game Christian was playing. His brother knew darn well who Lanni was. Good grief, he'd hired her!

He decided to ignore Christian, but his irritating younger brother would have none of it. Like a playful puppy, he followed them across to the room to where Ellen sat.

"Mother," Charles said, placing his arm around Lanni's shoulders, "this is Lanni Caldwell. Lanni, my mother, Ellen Greenleaf."

"Hello, Lanni."

"Hello." The two exchanged brief handshakes.

"Please sit down," Ellen said, patting the empty chair next to her. "Charles has told me very little about you."

Christian made a show of clearing his throat. "I know I'm stiff competition, but I still deserve an introduction," he insisted for the second time.

Charles frowned. "Don't tell me you don't recognize Lanni."

"I don't," Christian said blankly.

"She's Sawyer's secretary. You hired her, remember?"

Christian's look revealed his confusion. "I've never seen this woman before in my life."

"I think I can explain all this," Lanni said, her voice trembling slightly.

"The woman I hired as a secretary is named Mariah Douglas," Christian continued. "She arrives next week. I finished making the arrangements myself a couple of days ago."

Charles's frown deepened. "Lanni?"

"He's right," she said. Charles watched as her whole body tensed. "I came to Hard Luck to clean out my grandmother's house. Sawyer called my mother and asked if Midnight Sons could rent it."

"Your grandmother's house," Charles repeated.

"Catherine Fletcher is my grandmother," she said.

CHAPTER SIX

"CHARLES?" ELLEN TURNED to her son as if seeking an explanation. "Surely there's some mistake."

Charles ignored his mother, his deep blue eyes searing Lanni's. She squared her shoulders and met his gaze without flinching.

"There's no mistake, Mother," Charles said icily. "It seems I've been taken for a fool." With that he turned and walked away.

Lanni resisted the urge to run after him. "I apologize if I caused you any discomfort, Mrs. Greenleaf," she said calmly, doing her best to keep her voice void of emotion.

Ellen gazed after Charles. "I'm sorry, Lanni." Her eyes filled with sadness. "You see, there's been so much hurt to both families it's difficult to overlook. I don't wish your grandmother any harm, but at the same time I don't want anything to do with her, either."

"I understand." In essence Ellen was asking Lanni to leave. "I'm . . . glad to have met you."

Ellen didn't return the sentiment. Instead, she simply nodded.

With her heart in her throat, Lanni left Ellen and Christian. The need to talk this out with Charles burned in her chest. He was hurt and angry, justifiably so. But she hadn't meant to deceive him. She'd tried to tell him—twice—but both times he'd stopped her. She'd been almost grateful, fearing exactly this.

Lanni walked to the other side of the gymnasium and slumped weakly into a chair. It felt as if her feet would no longer hold her upright.

"Lanni, is something wrong?"

She glanced up to find Abbey standing over her. "Charles rushed out of here so fast," she went on.

"It's nothing," Lanni insisted, not wanting to ruin Abbey's wedding day with her own troubles.

Abbey took the vacant seat next to her. "I don't believe that. Now tell me what happened."

Lanni took a deep, stabilizing breath. "Charles learned that Catherine Fletcher's my grandmother. I should have told him from the first, but I didn't really think it would matter. I thought that once he got to know me he'd realize neither one of us has anything to do with the history between our families."

Abbey gave Lanni's hand a reassuring squeeze. "Give him time."

Lanni had already made that decision herself, although she thought she'd never forget the shock and anger in his eyes. The outrage seem to spit and boil inside him. He couldn't get away from her fast enough.

"Don't you worry about Charles and me," Lanni said, forcing herself to smile. "This is your day, and I don't want anything to spoil it."

"Nothing could," Abbey assured her. After a few more moments of low-key conversation, she rejoined her husband.

Lanni's throat felt dry and scratchy so she walked over to the punch bowl. She hadn't taken more than a sip of her sweet, fruity drink when Sawyer joined her.

"Abbey told me what happened," he said grimly.

"Charles needs time to get used to the idea, that's all," she said, making light of his reaction.

Sawyer eyes revealed his own remorse. "I should've told him."

"It wasn't your job."

"I purposely let him think you were the secretary Christian hired." A gathering frown darkened Sawyer's features. "Charles was so damn self-righteous when he learned what Christian and I had done to bring women to Hard Luck. When I realized how taken he was with you, I thought it was poetic justice. Frankly I felt it would do him good."

"I'm the one responsible," she argued gently, "not you."

"If you want, I'll talk to him."

As tempting as the offer was, Lanni refused to involve anyone else. "Thank you, but no. Either Charles and I work this out ourselves or we don't. It's not up to anyone else."

It pained her that Charles found it so difficult to accept her heritage. As Ellen had said earlier, sins were committed by both families. Lanni was willing to forgive what his family had done to hers, but apparently the reverse wasn't true.

"He's a stubborn cuss," Sawyer told her. "Be patient."

Lanni didn't answer. She had other commitments and responsibilities waiting for her in Anchorage. Within a matter of weeks, she was scheduled to start work with the newspaper. She wasn't willing to delay her return home, hoping Charles would magically come to his senses. He wasn't the only one who could be stubborn.

Sawyer left her and Lanni finished her punch. The drink felt cool and soothing against the tightness in her throat. Then, just as she was setting aside the empty crystal cup, she noticed Charles.

He'd come back to the reception. He stood on the other side of the room, as far away from her as he could get and still be in the same building. Intently his eyes followed her. She tried to smile, tried to tell him without words how very sorry she was.

The minute her eyes met his he turned and walked to his mother's side. The action told Lanni everything she needed to know. His loyalty rested with his family. He wanted nothing more to do with her.

"Hello, Lanni."

She looked up to find Duke Porter. "Hi, Duke."

"Would I get my head bitten off if I asked you to dance?"

"Of course not," she said.

"I didn't mean by you." Duke cast a look in Charles's direction. "You two seem to be an item. I don't want to cause problems, but Charles is sitting over there and you're here all alone—and you seem a little down in the mouth."

Pride elevated Lanni's chin. She had no idea others could see how miserable she was. "No one is going to object if we dance," she said, "least of all Charles O'Halloran."

ANGER POURED through Charles like liquid fire. Lanni hadn't been the only one to mislead him. Sawyer and Abbey had been in on this deception, too, making him the brunt of their joke. Still, he didn't fully blame Sawyer. His brother was so much in love he needed a compass to find his way to the john. Nor was Charles certain how much Abbey knew of the family history.

That left Lanni.

He might have been inclined to believe she was un-
aware of the facts, if it wasn't for one small thing. She'd
purposely led him to believe she was someone else. No
wonder she hadn't talked much about herself. He was
sure she knew. His stomach churned with rage, and it
was all he could do not to seek a release.

He'd made a first-class idiot of himself over Lanni
Caldwell. Granddaughter of the woman he hated. Earlier that afternoon he'd laid his heart at her feet. He
cringed when he remembered his disjointed speech
about falling in love with her. She must have been
snickering over that one!

Charles clung to his anger. It was necessary, otherwise those pleading looks she sent his way would dis-
solve the wall of grievances he'd built against her.

Unlike Lanni, he'd been old enough to remember
some of what happened. He'd seen with his own eyes
what Catherine Fletcher had done to his family. That
woman was responsible for ruining his parents' marriage, and his father's life. Charles would never forget
or forgive.

He turned away, unwilling to allow Lanni the satisfaction of knowing he was watching her. The determination to focus his attention elsewhere lasted all of two
minutes. When he sought her again, he found she
wasn't standing by the punch bowl.

Instead, she was dancing with Duke.

The anger brewing inside him intensified to glass-
melting degrees. The gentle sway of her hips was nearly
his undoing. The fact that Duke had his hand plastered
against those hips demanded every ounce of restraint he
possessed. He was a fraction of a heartbeat from butt-
ing his way through his brother's wedding guests and
plowing his fist halfway down Duke Porter's throat.

Even knowing what he did about Lanni couldn't keep Charles from wanting her. He'd never thought of himself as a weak man, but then, he hadn't known he was this much of a fool, either. What he needed, Charles decided, was a beer.

"Is everything all right?" Christian asked him.

Charles lifted the beer bottle to his lips. "Couldn't be better," he announced gruffly, unable to tear his gaze away from Lanni and Duke. It certainly hadn't taken her long to turn *her* attention to greener pastures.

"What's going on between you and Lanni?" Christian pressed.

"Not one damn thing." He wanted to tear off his brother's head for even asking.

"Peace, peace," Christian said, raising both hands. "All I did was ask a simple question."

"You got a simple answer."

Christian's gaze followed his. "She sure is a pretty thing," he murmured. "It's a damn shame she's related to Catherine." Having said that much, he wandered away. Charles was glad to be rid of him.

He wasn't in the mood for company, especially when it was his own brother reminding him how pretty Lanni was. He downed another swig of beer, but it did little to douse the burning anger.

Lanni loosely wrapped her arms around Duke's shoulders. The pilot's no-doubt clammy hands slid from the gentle swell of her hips to her waist and down again. That did it. Charles smacked the beer bottle down on the table and headed for the dance floor.

Sawyer waylaid him. "Do you have a problem?" he asked.

Charles glared at his brother. "Not really. Duke does. In another two minutes he's going to need a set of dentures."

"It's time you went outside and cooled down." Christian joined forces against Charles, and together, one at each side, his brothers escorted him out of the building.

The sun was so bright it nearly blinded him. "It isn't Duke you're angry with," Sawyer said evenly. "It's me. Only, I'm your brother and this is my wedding day."

Charles ground his teeth, recognizing the truth of his brother's words. He was angriest with Lanni, but that didn't completely absolve Sawyer of complicity in the deception.

"I should have told you."

Charles stiffened. "You're damn right you should have."

"I'll admit, it was a stupid trick. But frankly, Charles, does it matter who Lanni's related to? She didn't have anything to do with the past. She's her own woman. Judging her by Catherine's sins isn't fair, any more than it'd be fair if she blamed you for what Dad did."

"There are things you don't know!" Charles snapped. He wiped his face with a shaking hand in an effort to cool his temper. He knew far better than Sawyer or Christian the damage Catherine Fletcher had done to their family.

Every time he looked at Lanni he'd be reminded that she was a blood relative of Catherine's. He couldn't forget, and perhaps more importantly, he couldn't forgive.

"If that's the way he feels," Christian said to Sawyer, "then nothing we say is going to change his mind."

"I'm wondering, though," Sawyer said with a thoughtful frown, "if he can live with the consequences."

Charles threw his brothers a look that told them exactly where they could go and that he'd be more than happy to see to their arrival there.

"I'm getting out of here," Charles announced.

Sawyer and Christian exchanged looks.

"And I don't want or need any company, understand?" He had all the companionship he needed in the form of a bottle. He'd never purposely gotten drunk in his life. But there was a first time for everything.

LANNI SAW Charles disappear with his two brothers. Shortly afterward, Sawyer and Christian reappeared without him, and she didn't see him again. She tried to pretend it didn't matter, but couldn't hide the fact that it did.

Deciding to leave the reception herself, she found Abbey and Sawyer and hugged them both. "I hope you'll be very happy," she whispered, fearing her voice would break if she tried to speak normally. "My love goes with you."

"Everything will work out for the best," Abbey whispered in her ear.

Lanni managed a smile and nodded. "I'll remember that."

Sawyer's eyes were somber. "I'm sorry, Lanni."

"What for?" she asked with feigned cheerfulness. "You didn't do anything wrong." She was grateful he didn't offer her platitudes.

The reception broke up before Lanni could leave. Abbey and Sawyer were scheduled to fly into Fairbanks that evening, and then the following day take a flight to Honolulu for two glorious weeks in the sun. Abbey had mentioned earlier that Scott and Susan were flying out with their grandparents and that Charles would be looking after Eagle Catcher, Scott's husky. In the flurry of departures and teary goodbyes, Lanni quietly slipped off.

It seemed as though every ally she had in town was deserting her.

Her grandmother's house felt like a prison when she walked inside. Boxes lined one entire living room wall, ready to be mailed to Anchorage. That was something she'd learned soon after her arrival in Hard Luck—everything was sent via the United States Mail, even groceries. Transport by any other means was prohibitively expensive.

The phone rang, startling her. She stared at it until it rang again. With her heart hammering wildly, she grabbed the receiver.

"Hello," she said into the mouthpiece.

"Hiya there, little sister."

"Matt." Just the sound of his voice was comforting. "It's so good to hear from you."

"Miss me, do you?"

He hadn't a clue how much. She'd always idolized Matt; he'd been her knight in shining armor. Even when they were children, at an age when most siblings fought, Lanni had considered Matt as near perfect as it was possible for any human to be. Not until his marriage failed had Lanni found fault with him.

"So," Matt said, breaking into her thoughts, "you're hobnobbing with the O'Halloran brothers."

"Not exactly," she said, wanting to minimize her contact with Charles and his family.

"That's not what I hear. Mom said you filled in for Sawyer's secretary and that you mentioned meeting Charles."

"We've met." She swallowed painfully.

"According to Mom, you two have hit it off rather nicely."

Lanni's hand tightened around the telephone receiver. The temptation to spill her heart out to her older brother and seek his advice was almost overwhelming. But she wouldn't do that.

"Well, little sister, don't keep me in the dark."

She moistened her lips. "Charles is . . . a good man."

"Mom said you seemed quite enthralled with him."

"How's Karen?" Lanni asked in a desperate effort to change the subject. Then she sighed with regret—Matt had struggled with the breakup of his marriage. Lanni still worried about him. "I'm sorry, Matt. I can't seem to remember that you two aren't together any longer."

"Karen moved."

"Moved? What do you mean, she moved?"

"As in packed up her bags and headed south."

"How far south?"

"California."

Any hope Lanni still harbored of a reconciliation between her brother and his wife was dashed. With Karen living thousands of miles from Anchorage, the likelihood of those two settling their differences seemed almost nil.

"When did that happen?" Lanni generally stayed in close contact with Karen, and she hadn't heard a word about her leaving Alaska.

"Last week. Paragon, Inc. offered her a giant promotion. Unfortunately it entailed a transfer. From what I understand, she leapt at the chance. Naturally she didn't call to talk it over with me. I heard through the grapevine that she packed up and was out of here in two days flat."

Lanni's eyes drifted shut. No wonder her brother didn't recognize her anguish; he was dealing with his own.

"I'm sorry to hear that."

"Mom said Karen tried to contact you before she left." *But not Matt.* "I want only the best for her." He said the words as if by rote. Lanni knew he didn't dare admit—least of all to himself—how much he loved and missed his ex-wife; admitting it would leave him too vulnerable, too ravaged. "Only the best," he said again.

"I know you do, Matt."

"Listen," he said, brightening, "I didn't call to get us both down in the doldrums."

"Good." Lanni could do with a bit of cheering up.

"I heard a rumor I want you to check out for me."

"Sure."

"Is it true there's some kind of lodge in Hard Luck?"

"Yes, sort of. There was a fire some years back that burned part of it. No one ever bothered to repair it."

"That's great!"

"Great? If you want the truth, I wonder why Charles's family hasn't torn it down by now. The place is completely boarded up. My feeling is it needs to be either rebuilt or destroyed."

"Do you think they'd be willing to sell it?"

"The lodge?"

"Of course the lodge."

"Why?" It made no sense to Lanni.

"Why?" her brother repeated.

It was beginning to sound as if the phone had developed an echo. "Because I'd like a chance to do something with it. Gate of the Arctic National Park's close by, isn't it? The lodge would be perfect tourist accommodation.''

Tourist accommodation? Her brother must have lost every shred of reason he'd ever possessed. "But, Matt, what about the winters? What tourist in his right mind would visit the Arctic in December and January? You'd go broke."

"Dogs, Lanni. There are hundreds of adventure-seekers out there looking for a new thrill. I'll take them mushing. Just look at the popularity of the Iditarod and some of the other races."

"But you'd have to raise the dogs first." Surely this project would cost more than he could possibly afford.

"Not necessarily. I'll rent them and whatever else I need from the pros. This is the opportunity of a life-time, Lanni, and I'm getting in on the ground floor."

Briefly Lanni wondered if her brother really had lost his mind. He routinely came up with these crazy ideas, but this was the craziest yet. None of them held his attention for long. He'd get started on some fabulous plan, some wonderful new career that was sure to make him rich, and tire of it within six months. Lanni had seen the pattern countless times.

"Ask Charles for me, would you, Lanni?"

Lanni pressed her hand to her forehead. "No..." She'd never refused her brother anything. Until now.

"No?"

"If you're truly interested in buying that burned-out lodge from the O'Halloran brothers, then you can ask them yourself."

Her words were followed by a lengthy pause. "Lanni, is everything all right?"

"It's peachy keen," she lied. "Just wonderful. I'm nearly finished with Grammy's house. I might even manage to be home in a couple of days."

"You don't sound so good," Matt said gently. "You'd better tell me what's happened."

"Nothing's happened."

"You're sure?"

"Positive. Just answer me one question."

"Anything."

She took a shaky breath. "Are all men born bastards, or do they have to work hard to achieve it?"

Matt chuckled. "You've locked horns with the O'Hallorans, have you?"

"Something like that."

"Well, I don't know about the O'Hallorans, but I guess the answer depends on who you ask. Karen would agree I'm a bastard, and she'd tell you I worked hard to achieve it. But I gotta say I seem to have came by the talent naturally."

LURING WOMEN to Hard Luck wasn't working out the way Christian had speculated. One brother was married and the other wasn't speaking to him.

Since he'd been away from his desk for so long, Christian decided to walk down to the airfield and check out the office.

The morning was clear and bright. Abbey and Sawyer and their entourage had gotten off safely the day before. The kids and their grandparents had left today. Christian glanced at his watch. By now the honeymoon couple would be on a plane headed for beautiful Waikiki.

Christian was about to step up to the mobile office when he heard the buzz of an approaching aircraft.

None of Midnight Sons' planes was in the air, which meant that another of the flying services was making a run into Hard Luck. He stood outside the trailer and watched the descent of the single-engine aircraft.

Frontier was a well-known flight-service contractor flying out of Fairbanks. The pilots made regular stops in Hard Luck. Only this wasn't one of their routine runs.

The Cessna landed, coasting to a stop.

The door lowered, and a young woman with soft red hair cautiously descended. She paused when she stepped onto the runway, apparently surveying the town.

Christian was sure he recognized her, but he couldn't recall exactly when they'd met or where. In the past five weeks, he'd interviewed more women than he cared to count.

The plane's engine continued to purr in the early-morning stillness. The pilot handed the redhead a piece of luggage, which she promptly dropped. Her expensive-looking suitcase hit the ground and snapped open.

At least half a dozen pairs of lacy panties spilled onto the dirt-and-gravel runway. The whirling blades of the Cessna created a strong breeze. The woman gave a frustrated cry and chased after her underwear, leaving the suitcase open. The wind caught on several other items, lifting them from the neatly folded stack of unmentionables.

A second suitcase appeared while the woman chased hither and yon.

Christian would have volunteered to help, but he strongly suspected his effort wouldn't be appreciated.

The woman snatched up a delicate black bra and several other skimpy items, then hurriedly stuffed them back into the suitcase, slamming it closed.

Christian resisted the urge to laugh.

The redhead managed to retrieve everything. She lifted the suitcase and carried it awkwardly under her arm. One bra strap and several lacy odds and ends dangled from the sides.

The Frontier pilot spoke to her for a few minutes, then they solemnly shook hands and he prepared to leave. She waved enthusiastically as the plane began its takeoff.

"Hello," she said, smiling brightly when she saw Christian.

"Hello," he answered, stepping forward. "Would you like some help with your luggage?"

"No thanks, I've got everything under control." With some difficulty she looped her purse strap over her shoulder and lifted the second suitcase.

"Welcome to Hard Luck." Christian still hadn't figured out where he'd met his woman.

"I can't tell you how good it is to finally get here," she said, sighing. "I had no idea how far from civilization this place is."

Although she claimed she didn't want any help, she was obviously in need of it. He removed the suitcases from her hands.

"I hope it isn't a problem that I arrived a day early," she said.

"A day early?"

"Yes. I'm Mariah Douglas, the secretary you hired. Don't you remember?"

LANNI HAD NEVER SPENT a more miserable day in her life. She worked all morning and afternoon, sorting through Grammy's personal items. When she happened upon a thick manila envelope tucked in the back of the bookcase, she suspected it had something to do with David O'Halloran. She was right.

Inside she discovered the letters he'd mailed her from Europe during the war. Lanni fingered them, but hadn't the heart to read them. For more than fifty years, her grandmother had saved love letters from a man who'd betrayed her.

Lanni hadn't eaten all day, and she decided a walk would do her good.

Burying her hands deep in her sweater pockets, she started toward the Hard Luck Café. As she turned off Main Street, she saw Charles walking toward her. Her first inclination was to ignore him, to pretend she hadn't seen him.

He'd obviously recognized her the same moment she saw him. His step faltered slightly, as if the mere sight of her was enough to knock him off balance.

They continued toward each other at the same slow pace, their gazes wary, until only a few feet separated them. Lanni spoke first. "Charles, please . . ."

"What?" he asked gruffly.

"If I misled you, I'm sorry."

"*If?*" he said.

The silence stretched between them.

"I assume you're looking for an apology," she finally said, trying one last time, "and I'll admit I was wrong. I should have told you the first time we met, but I was hoping that once you got to know me you'd be willing to put old grievances aside." She struggled to keep the hurt out of her voice.

He gave a smile that lacked any hint of amusement.

Lanni could feel her anger take hold. She pointed a finger at Charles. "Something is very wrong here. *Your* father left *my* grandmother standing at the altar fifty years ago, and *I'm* the one apologizing to *you.*''

Charles's eyes flared, but he said nothing.

''You know what I found this morning?'' Of course he didn't, but she was going to tell him. ''Letters. My grandmother kept the letters your father wrote her while he was away at war. All these years she's treasured them. I found them with ribbons wrapped around them hidden in the back of her bookcase.''

Charles clenched his fists at his sides. ''Your grandmother ruined my father's life.''

''Oh, please. He did it to himself.''

''There are things you don't know.''

''I know enough. My grandmother was so much in love with him she went down to Fairbanks and had her photograph taken in her wedding dress—the one she intended to wear for him. Can you imagine how she must have felt when she learned he'd married someone else? Do you have any idea how difficult it is to stop loving someone?''

Fire leapt into his eyes, but he said nothing.

''What is this?'' she shouted in frustration. ''A family trait.''

''What the hell are you talking about now?''

Lanni's nails bit into the tender flesh of her palms. ''You,'' she said, unable to conceal her emotion any longer. ''Did you or did you not claim you loved me? Apparently the words mean nothing to an O'Halloran. Not to your father, not to you.''

She thought she saw regret flash in his eyes, but he didn't speak.

''I see,'' she said softly.

''You should have told me who you were,'' he mumbled at last.

"I did," she returned stiffly.

"You didn't."

She held her hand over her heart. "I'm Lanni Caldwell. What more would you need to know?"

He closed his eyes as if to block her out.

Swallowing her pride, Lanni tried one more time. "What happened, happened. It's true my grandmother was no saint, but then neither was your father. And, Charles, neither are you. Neither am I."

"I'm sorry, Lanni," he said, pushing back his dark hair with one hand.

"Sorry?" She didn't understand. "What are you saying?" It came to her then with a sickening sense of dread. "Charles," she whispered, her voice catching, "what are you saying?"

He sucked in a deep breath.

"You don't want anything to do with me?"

He nodded slowly.

Anger and frustration boiled inside her. "Then say it!" she shouted. "At least have the courage to say it to my face."

The pain in his eyes was almost more than she could bear. He lifted his arm and gently stroked her face. "It was never meant to be, Lanni. Not for us."

CHAPTER SEVEN

LANNI HAD TOLD Charles she'd studied journalism. He sat nursing his coffee in the Hard Luck Café, mulling over what had happened between him and Lanni. Mitch Harris, who worked for the Department of the Interior, and his daughter, Chrissie, sat at one of the tables, having breakfast.

He remembered the day he'd taken her to his grandfather's original claim, when they'd sat by the camp stove and talked. He'd wondered at the time what she was doing working as a secretary if she had a journalism degree under her belt. The truth was, he hadn't cared. He was so damn glad she was in Hard Luck he hadn't questioned the why or wherefores.

Since the wedding reception, recriminations had been coming at him from all directions. Even Ben seemed ready to take him to task.

"Ready for a refill?" Ben stopped at the table, coffeepot in hand.

Charles stared down at his cup, the coffee long since gone lukewarm. "No thanks."

Ben lingered. "Normally I don't butt into someone else's business unless I'm asked, but—"

"I'd advise you to do the same now," Charles said evenly. He'd been friends with Ben for a good many years. He didn't want that relationship ruined now, especially over Lanni.

"I'd keep my trap shut if it weren't for one thing." Ben set the coffeepot on the table, and glancing over at Mitch, lowered his voice. "I told you about Marilyn. I haven't said her name aloud in ten, maybe fifteen years. Talking about her stirred up a lot of old feelings that should've stayed at rest. The way I figure it, you owe me."

"I owe you for the coffee, nothing else."

"Not this time, Charlie."

No one called him Charlie. Ben knew that.

"Lanni's leaving town," Ben said. "I heard her make the arrangements."

"I know." What did Ben think he'd been doing for the last thirty minutes? Charles had been sitting there, trying to figure out where he was going to find the strength to let her walk out of his life.

Ben's mouth thinned. "You know?"

Charles's hand tightened around his mug until his knuckles showed white. "It's inevitable, don't you think?"

The older man didn't answer. "You're going to let her?"

Charles expelled his breath forcefully and nodded.

Ben cocked his head to one side as if he couldn't believe what he'd heard. Or, more to the point, as if he simply hadn't *liked* what he'd heard. "You mean to say you're actually going to let Lanni Caldwell walk out of your life even after what I told you?" Ben sounded incredulous. "If you do anything so damn stupid, I guarantee you're going to regret this the rest of your life."

"Maybe."

"Okay, so you don't owe me anything, but what do you owe yourself? Lanni, too. She deserves better than this. Maybe you're just looking for an excuse to be rid of her. That's what it sounds like to me."

"Stay out of this, Ben," Charles warned. "What happens between Lanni and me isn't any of your damned business."

"I don't understand it," Ben muttered, slowly shaking his head. "I really don't understand it." He picked up the coffeepot and walked back to the kitchen. "College-educated, smart as a tack when it comes to book learning, yet I've never met a more stupid, more stubborn—"

"Bastard," Charles supplied for him.

Ben just shook his head.

It was useless for Charles to explain that there were certain elements of his relationship with Lanni that Ben couldn't possibly understand.

"One last word of advice," Ben called. "I'm telling you this because I know." He splayed his fingers across his chest. "I've lived with my mistakes for the past twenty-five years. I didn't know when I refused to read Marilyn's letters that we wouldn't see each other again. There was never anyone else for me, Charles. Think about that. Would you let Lanni go if you knew you'd never see her again?"

"Yes. I would." Charles stood up and slapped a fistful of change on the table, then walked out of the café.

DUKE PORTER was due to arrive with the Midnight Sons' truck shortly after noon. Lanni was ready for him. She'd transferred the boxes from the living room onto the porch, then she sat on the top step to wait. Her muscles ached, but she welcomed the physical pain.

A plume of dust appeared in the distance. Wiping the perspiration from her brow with the back of her wrist, she got to her feet, assuming it was Duke. She quickly realized she was wrong—it was Charles driving past. He kept his eyes trained ahead, avoiding even a glance in her direction. For all the notice he gave her, she might as well have been invisible.

Lanni sank back onto the step, struggling with her emotions. She covered her face with her hands and drew in one deep breath after another in an effort to distance the pain.

How often, she wondered, had her grandmother's heart raced at the sound of an approaching car? Had David come to her? Ever? All those years she'd waited for him. Hoped. Pined. Suffered. Now Grammy was dying, and Lanni knew why. The doctors had their reasons. They said it was her heart. In a manner of speaking they were right. Her grandmother had been slowly dying for the past ten years because she had no reason to continue living. David, the man she'd loved from the time she was a teenager, was dead. The only hope she had of ever being with him again lay on the other side of life.

Like his father before him, Charles wasn't free to love her. But it wasn't another woman who stood between her and Charles. Family loyalty was what had destroyed their love. Now Charles wanted nothing to do with her.

Unlike her grandmother, Lanni would leave voluntarily. But not without pain or regret. Head held high, unwilling to apologize for who she was, she would walk away.

Duke pulled up a few minutes later and loaded the truck himself. She signed the necessary papers, gave him an address to send the final bill to and returned to the house.

In the morning she'd leave Hard Luck.

Her last night in town, Lanni sat on the swing on her grandmother's front porch. A gentle breeze, scented with tundra wildflowers, stirred restlessly. Lanni closed her eyes and recalled the last time she'd sat on a swing. A child's swing, very different from this one. A night very different from this one, too....

Lanni basked in the comfortable silence. She listened to the crickets, the birds, the sounds of evening—an evening as bright as noontime—searching for solace she knew she wouldn't find.

She didn't understand how her grandmother could have remained in Hard Luck waiting for a man who would never love her. Year after year, until she was old and bitter.

How miserable she must have been.

Lanni closed her eyes. These final hours in town were agony for her. Yet Catherine had stayed on year after year, never giving up hope that one day David would be hers again.

The sound of approaching footsteps alerted her to the fact that she was no longer alone.

Lanni opened her eyes to discover Charles standing on the other side of the white picket fence that framed her grandmother's yard. Her pulse quickened.

Was he real or some figment of her imagination? Had this happened to Grammy, too? Had she been so desperate for David that she'd pictured him coming to her the way Lanni was seeing Charles?

"I shouldn't be here."

So he was real. One look told her he hadn't wanted to come. His eyes were filled with pain. He turned to leave.

She rushed down the steps to the walk. "Don't go."

He hesitated.

"Come sit with me," she invited, gesturing toward the swing.

Charles moved closer. Watching him, she could almost see the battle being waged inside him. She realized he didn't understand what had driven him to her. She suspected he considered it a deficiency of character, a weakness. If that was the case, then she was weak too.

Lanni turned to climb the steps again and sat where she'd been sitting moments earlier, on the swing, leaving space beside her.

Charles opened the gate and came through. He climbed the steps, too, but paused at the top. Nothing showed in his face; nevertheless Lanni could tell how tightly he reined in his emotions.

"I'm not as different from my father as I thought," he said hoarsely. "He couldn't stay away, either."

Lanni didn't understand, but she wasn't sure it mattered. Not right now. Charles was here, with her, on her last night in Hard Luck.

She drank in the sight of him. She felt a jolt of pain when she saw the lines about his eyes and the rigid way he held himself. He was hurting, just as she was.

"Years ago," he continued in an emotionless voice, "my mother returned to England. She took Christian with her. My father was devastated. At first he found comfort in the bottle, but that didn't last long. He never was much of a drinking man."

Charles paused, rubbing his hand along the back of his neck. "Later it was Catherine who...comforted him."

If that was true, Lanni couldn't understand why Charles hated her grandmother so much. She didn't know whether to be shocked—or pleased that Catherine had even a little time with the man she loved.

"Dad didn't think Sawyer or I knew where he went nights," he said. "But we did. We never talked about it. Catherine became like an addiction to him."

"That was a long time ago."

"He couldn't stay away from Catherine, and I can't stay away from you." It sounded like a confession. "I haven't the strength to resist you, Lanni."

She stood, causing the swing to sway gently behind her. Wordlessly she walked over to him and touched his face. "I love you, Charles."

He pulled her toward him, urgently seeking her mouth. Again and again he kissed her as if he couldn't get enough. Intuitively she realized that whatever she gave him now would need to last them both a lifetime.

Charles buried his fingers in her hair and groaned.

She slipped her arms around his neck, pressing herself against him. He drew in a swift breath and kissed her again with an intensity that left her reeling.

Then he caught hold of her arms and pulled them down to her sides. "No more," he said roughly. "We can't do this..."

Lanni hugged herself against him, molding her body to his. The quick surge of his heart, the hardening of his body, told her what she needed to know. After a moment she felt his hand move lightly on her hair.

She eased out of his embrace and led him into the house, her heart beating heavily. He turned to close the door.

"Just hold me," she told him in a whisper, nestling in his arms. "That's all I want. All I'll ever ask."

They sat on the sofa, the same one her grandmother must have sat on with his father. Charles seemed to realize this at the precise moment she did.

"My father was with Catherine—here."

"I know. We can move," she said quickly.

"It's not important." When he brought her back into his embrace, his touch was tender. He kissed her face, her eyes and nose and chin. His mouth was gentle over hers, drinking in her love. Lanni's heart fluttered with excitement, with passion. With hope.

Easing away from her, he unfastened the row of buttons and spread open her blouse. He stopped, his breathing ragged. Lanni reached behind her and unsnapped her bra, freeing her breasts. He inhaled sharply, then lowered his mouth to kiss each one.

When he raised his head he was trembling. Lanni loved him all the more for his restraint. He cupped her breasts and then slowly, lovingly, explored the swell and curve of each.

"We have to stop," he whispered in a voice she barely recognized as his.

She nodded. Her fingers refused to cooperate as she fumbled with the buttons on her blouse. Charles tried to help her, but his efforts proved just as inept. They both gave up, and Lanni pulled the edges of the blouse together, holding them closed.

Charles settled back on the sofa. He gathered Lanni to him, her back against his chest.

"Tell me what you meant earlier," she said when she found her voice. "About David not being able to stay away from Catherine."

"They had an affair," Charles answered, and breathed softly into her hair. "Maybe it wasn't such a big deal...."

"You haven't forgotten. Neither has your mother." She leaned back far enough so she could look into his eyes.

He didn't answer her, not right away. His arms, still holding her, tightened slightly. "Eventually we received word that Ellen was returning to Alaska. To Hard Luck. She didn't want the divorce. She wanted to come home."

Lanni closed her eyes, thinking of two teenage boys eager to have their mother back. At the same time she understood how the news must have crushed her grandmother.

"My father had to tell Catherine. She'd come to our house—I was doing my homework in the kitchen at the time." He paused. "Catherine was hysterical. She yelled and screamed and repeatedly hit my father. He didn't even attempt to defend himself, and he stopped me when I tried to intervene. I'd come running in when I heard the noise. Thank heaven Sawyer wasn't there. Again and again Catherine told him he couldn't do this to her. Not again. Not a second time."

Lanni's eyes flooded with tears.

"She started sobbing. She told Dad he'd be sorry, and then she ran out the door."

Charles's fingers bit into her arms. Lanni was sure he didn't realize how strong his grip was.

"After she left—" he hesitated "—Dad broke down. It's the only time in my life I ever saw him weep. At first I thought she might have physically hurt him. Only later did I realize what was wrong."

He stopped, as if the telling was too much.

"I need to know. Please, Charles, just tell me," Lanni pleaded.

"He wept because he loved Catherine. He'd always loved her."

"Then why..." Lanni was confused. If David had truly cared for Catherine, why had he taken Ellen back?

Charles understood her unfinished question. "I'd like to think my father loved my mother, too," he whispered. "My brothers think so, but I don't know. I just don't know. They'd been married nearly twenty-five years by that time. Ellen had no one. Except her sons. Her family had been dead for years, wiped out in the war, and when she returned to England there was no one there for her. All the years she lived in Alaska she'd built up a fantasy of what her life would've been like in England. But when she went back, she discovered she wasn't happy there, either."

"How long was she away?"

"Eighteen months."

Poor Ellen. She belonged to two different worlds, but to neither one completely.

"Mother missed Sawyer and me, and wanted another chance to make her marriage work. To her credit she tried hard. For a while after her return she was involved in the community, volunteered at the school, that sort of thing."

"Until?"

Charles's hands caressed her forearms. "Until Catherine made good on her threat."

Lanni stiffened.

"Catherine made my mother the town laughing-stock. The first thing she did was tell Ellen about her affair with my father. She supplied plenty of details, too. And she made sure everyone in Hard Luck heard the whole story. More important, she took delight in purposely destroying whatever chance my parents had of making their marriage work."

"You hate my grandmother, don't you?"

"Yes." Charles didn't hesitate. "My mother made plenty of mistakes over the years, but she didn't deserve that.

"She'd done nothing wrong except to fall in love with a man who loved someone else. I'll never understand why they married in the first place. Although, I guess people often behave very differently in wartime than they otherwise would."

"Your father allowed Catherine to taunt Ellen?"

Charles didn't answer her question. "Catherine wasn't content with making Ellen miserable. She did whatever she could to hurt my father, as well. Remember the old saying 'Hell hath no fury like a woman scorned'? I swear Catherine Fletcher was the most bitter woman there ever was.

"My father betrayed my mother with his affair, and then Catherine humiliated her. I can't hurt her again. I refuse to be involved with someone who'll be a constant reminder of the woman who brought so much pain into her life."

Lanni jerked herself free of Charles's embrace. She moved off the sofa, still clutching her blouse with one hand. "What about *my* grandmother? Don't you think *she* deserved better? Twice your father used her. Twice he cast her aside. Can you blame her? Can you honestly blame her? You claim he loved her. I doubt it. He did nothing but use her!"

Charles didn't answer, not that she expected him to. With hands trembling so badly she found it difficult to lift her arm, Lanni brushed away the hair that had fallen in her face.

"You say my grandmother ruined your father's marriage and his life. I wonder." She paused and inhaled deeply. "I wonder if you've considered what he did to her. She married shortly after he returned from the war with his bride, but that marriage didn't last more than two years.

"She gave up custody of her only child so she could remain close to David. Catherine is a stranger to my mother. A stranger to me. All because of your father."

Leaning forward, Charles braced his elbows against his knees and hung his head. "Now you know why there can never be anything between us," he whispered.

Lanni stood stiffly beside him. "I'm sorry, Charles, for the pain my family caused yours. And the pain yours has caused mine."

"I'm sorry, too. For all of it."

"But it doesn't change anything."

He shook his head. "Your leaving is for the best."

She fought to keep her voice even. "I'm not going to make the mistakes my grandmother did," she told him, her voice quavering despite her efforts. "I'm not going to spend the rest of my life pining away for you."

"I wouldn't want that."

"I'm going back to Anchorage and I'll do my damnedest to forget I ever met you." Using the back of one hand, she swiped at the tears running down her face.

He gave a brief nod of his head.

"I'm not coming back to Hard Luck again." She swiped at her face again, hating the weakness that let the tears fall. Slowly she backed away from him.

Charles stood up, raking his hand through his hair. "I thought you should know," he said.

She lowered her head. "It helps. Now that I've been properly informed, everything's evened out. I can hate your family, too."

He turned and, his shoulders hunched, walked out of her life.

This time, she knew, it was forever.

SAWYER SAT PROPPED against the headboard, and Abbey was leaning against him, her face resting on his hair-roughened chest. The sound of the surf persistently pounding the beach came from the open lanai. A tropical breeze rustled through the palm trees just outside.

"Eventually we're going to have to leave this room," Abbey said with a sigh.

Sawyer stroked her hair. "Why?"

Abbey rolled back her head to look into her husband's clear gray-blue eyes. "In case you haven't noticed, paradise is right outside that sliding-glass door."

"Paradise is being right here with you."

Not for the first time, Abbey marveled at her husband's romantic heart. This side of Sawyer had come as a pleasant surprise—along with what she'd learned about his sensual nature. Marriage to Sawyer was going to be a wonderful adventure.

The first night of their honeymoon, in Fairbanks, they'd made love again and again, before falling asleep in each other's arms. The next morning, they were on a flight to Hawaii.

When they arrived, all Abbey wanted was a feather pillow and a bed. Sawyer was interested in a bed, too, but not for the purpose of sleep. This man she'd married, Abbey soon discovered, was inexhaustible. Their dinner had been delivered to the room, followed by a late breakfast some hours later. Still they lingered in bed.

"I'd like to play tourist for a while," she said. "Would you mind?"

Sawyer ran his hand down her bare back. He released a slow, long-suffering sigh. "I suppose I could manage to drag myself out of bed, but only if you promise one thing."

"What's that?"

"You'll feed me."

Abbey looked toward the bedside clock. "Don't tell me it's lunchtime already."

"I was referring to a different appetite." A sexy smile played on his lips. "It isn't a plate of meat and potatoes that interests me. I'm thinking more along the lines of . . . dessert."

"Now?" What she really meant was, "Again?"

"There's no time like the present." He slanted his mouth over hers, and Abbey groaned, sliding toward him.

"Sawyer," she protested without any real fervor, "it's already ten-thirty and—"

"You're right," he said, pressing her down onto the mattress and bending over her. "It's much too late to get started today. We'll have to wait until tomorrow to explore the island."

Abbey giggled. "That wasn't what I meant."

His tongue slid across her lips.

"Then again . . ." she said breathlessly, "you might be right."

His tongue probed hers. "I thought you'd see the error or your ways."

Eventually they did leave the room. Abbey even managed to convince Sawyer to purchase them matching shirts and straw hats in the hotel gift shop.

"I look like I'm wearing a pineapple," he complained, studying himself in the shop mirror.

Abbey laughed, feeling lighthearted and very much in love.

Sawyer rented a car and they drove to the north shore of Oahu. They discovered a deserted beach and lay there soaking up the sunshine. Abbey had him spread suntan lotion on her back.

"Do you need any help with the front?" he asked eagerly.

"No." She squeezed the lotion onto her arms and rubbed it vigorously into her pale skin. She paused when she found Sawyer watching her every move.

"Will you stop?" she asked.

"Stop what?"

"Looking at me like that."

His face revealed complete innocence. "Like what?"

Abbey rolled her eyes. "Like you're going to ravish me the first chance you get."

He lowered his sunglasses, his eyes devilish. "That's exactly what I intend, woman."

Abbey smiled. Although she'd been married before, she'd never felt this loved or cherished. And she'd never felt this sexy. "It'd serve you right if I turned up pregnant after this honeymoon," she told him absently, snapping closed the lid on the bottle of suntan lotion.

Sawyer went still. "Is there a chance?"

She glanced at him, fearing his reaction to the truth. They hadn't talked about birth control. "Yes," she whispered. "There wasn't time for me to start on the pill, and we . . . we haven't stopped long enough for any precautions."

Sawyer let out a shout of sheer delight and sent his hat flying toward the cloudless blue sky. "Hot damn, woman, if I'd known that we'd *never* have left the hotel room."

"You mean to say you wouldn't object?"

"Object? If you were to get pregnant on this trip it would be the second-best thing that ever happened to me."

"What's the first?"

He seemed surprised she didn't know. "Meeting you, my love, what else?"

Abbey leapt up from the beach towel and stuffed it into her bag. Once that was finished, she shoved in everything else she'd so carefully unpacked.

"Come on," she said to her husband.

He looked at her as if he didn't know what to make of her abrupt movements. "Where are we going?"

She blinked. "Back to the hotel room of course!"

LANNI STOPPED at the Hard Luck Café on her way to the airfield early the following morning.

"Morning, Ben," she said, slipping the backpack off her shoulders and setting it aside.

"Morning." He eyed her bags. "It looks to me like you're getting ready to head out of here."

She smiled sadly. "I thought I'd come in for one last cup of coffee and to tell you goodbye." She held out her hand to him.

He shook it, his hand firmly clasping hers.

"We're going to miss you around here," Ben said.

"I'm going to miss you, too."

"Miss me? My guess is I'm not the one you're really going to yearn for once you're back home."

She lowered her head, refusing to react to his comment. "Well, I have to say it's been interesting."

"Yup, I suppose it has."

He poured her a cup of coffee and she reached for her purse.

Ben shook his head. "On the house."

"Thanks." She sipped the coffee, needing it. She hadn't slept much and hoped the coffee would revive her enough to see her through the morning.

"It's a damn shame about you and Charles."

She shrugged as if their relationship mattered little. "You win some, you lose some."

"You fit in this town a hell of a lot better than some of those women Christian hired. One of them didn't stay long enough to give it a chance. Another woman—a teacher—wouldn't even get off the plane."

"You're joking!"

"It's true," he said, leaning both hands on the counter. "Ask anyone."

"I believe you."

"Damn shame you have to go back."

She didn't contradict him.

"Who's flying you into Fairbanks?"

"Ralph," she answered. He wasn't one of the pilots she'd gotten to know. She checked her watch. "I better get on over to the office before they take off without me."

"We're gonna miss you, Lanni," Ben said again as she collected her bags.

Blinking fiercely to force back the tears, she raised her hand in farewell and hurried out the door.

Charles's truck, loaded with camping equipment, was parked in front of the mobile office. She hesitated, reluctant to go in, until she recognized Ralph, who stood just inside the door. He looked up from his clipboard and grinned when he saw her.

"I'm just about ready," he called. "Go ahead and get on the plane."

The office door opened and Charles walked out. He stopped abruptly when he saw her.

Lanni looked longingly toward the plane. They'd said their farewells; there was nothing more to say.

"Goodbye, Charles," she said, holding out her hand in a businesslike manner.

He stared at it for a moment, then his fingers closed convulsively over hers. "Goodbye, Lanni."

She offered him a proud smile and turned away. Climbing into the plane, she took her seat and snapped the belt into place.

With tears burning in her eyes and threatening to fall, she looked out the small window to find Charles standing next to his truck, watching her. He didn't move.

Ralph put her luggage aboard and climbed in. He reviewed the safety instructions with her, although she wasn't listening, then started the engine.

Lanni kept her eyes trained on Charles. Her face was pressed to the window as the engine roared to life.

The plane taxied down the runway.

Lanni craned her neck as far as possible in order to watch Charles.

He stepped forward a few paces, then stopped. She stared out the window until he disappeared from view.

CHAPTER EIGHT

"HELLO, GRAMMY, it's me. Lanni." Catherine Fletcher gave Lanni an odd look, as though she didn't recognize her.

Catherine was in her early seventies, but she looked older. There were deeply etched lines of bitterness around her mouth and eyes. "I know who you are. Where's Kate?"

"Mom's coming."

"Your mother hasn't been to see me all week. If my daughter is going to shuffle me off to die, the least she can do is come visit."

Lanni knew her mother had been to the nursing home practically every day. The burden of these daily visits had taken their toll on her. Yet Kate remained faithful, doing whatever she could to make Catherine as comfortable as possible.

"Well, don't just stand there," Catherine said sourly. "Bring me my robe. I want out of this blasted bed."

For all her blustering, Lanni's grandmother was as fragile as a spider's web. She was thinner than Lanni remembered and terribly frail.

"Mother, you know you can't get out of bed without a nurse's assistance." Kate stood in the doorway, her voice filled with concern and frustration. "And there's no reason to snap at Lanni."

Lanni was greatly relieved that her mother had chosen that moment to arrive.

Catherine looked away sheepishly.

"I thought we'd wash and dry your hair this afternoon," Kate said, her tone gentler. Catherine's hair was tied at the back of her neck, but the frizzy sides stuck out in every direction. "We've let it go for several days now."

Catherine pinched her lips with disapproval.

"I wish you'd allow someone to cut it," Kate went on.

"No," came Catherine's sharp retort. "No one's touching my hair but me."

"Whatever you say, Mother."

Lanni marveled at her mother's patience.

An hour later she accompanied Kate out of the nursing home. "How do you do it?" she asked, amazed at her mother's tender care for a woman who seemed so mean-spirited.

"She's my mother," Kate explained simply. "She wasn't the best mother in the world, but I suppose she wasn't the worst, either. Adjusting to life in the nursing home is difficult for her. We need to remember that Catherine was independent all those years."

"But she's so..."

"Ungrateful?" Kate supplied.

"Yes."

"She doesn't mean to be," Kate said. "Mother's miserable. I don't think she's had much happiness in her life. Her health is failing, and I fear we won't have her much longer. I don't want any regrets when the time comes to bury her."

Lanni understood what her mother meant about regrets. She felt trapped in a mire of her own might-havebeens. Not a minute passed that she didn't think of Charles. Since her return to Anchorage, Lanni felt constantly on the verge of tears.

"Are you ready for lunch?" Kate asked, linking her arm with Lanni's.

Lanni nodded, managing a smile.

"Good."

Kate took Lanni to her favorite seafood place. Generally Lanni was treated to this particular restaurant only for special occasions like her birthday.

They were seated in a comfortable upholstered booth; it was situated in front of a window overlooking Turnagain Arm, an elongated waterway that extended from Cook Inlet. If Lanni remembered her history correctly, Turnagain Arm had been discovered by Captain James Cook on his third and final voyage in 1778 while he was searching for the Northwest Passage. The unusual name was because Cook and his crew had had to turn back yet again.

"Are we celebrating something?" Lanni asked, surprised by her mother's choice of restaurants. She spread the linen napkin across her lap.

"You're home."

"I've been back almost a month." Twenty-seven days to be exact. Every minute of those days had felt like a year to Lanni. It amazed her that she could have known Charles so briefly and yet love him so intently. Every day without him was a struggle; her appetite was nonexistent, and she wasn't sleeping well.

"Something happened while you were in Hard Luck," her mother said quietly, studying Lanni over the top of the menu. "You haven't said anything, but it's obvious to your father and me that you're unhappy."

"It's nothing, Mom. I'm fine."

"You've lost weight, and Lanni... Oh, sweetheart, I want you to know that there isn't *anything* you can't tell me. I'm your mother, and if I can't help you, I'll find someone who can. Please tell me what's troubling you."

Lanni had always felt close to her mother, but never more than right at that moment. She'd watched her deal effectively with her own mother's bitterness and was deeply impressed by what a good daughter she was. Now Kate was proving once again that she was an equally good mother.

"It's almost embarrassing to say," Lanni began, crumpling in her fist the napkin she'd so recently smoothed. "I fell in love. Unfortunately the man I fell in love with is... Charles O'Halloran."

Her mother's eyes closed. "David O'Halloran's son?"

"Yes," Lanni whispered. "You told me some of what happened between David and Grammy, and Charles filled in the rest."

"Perhaps someday you can tell me what you learned. There's a lot I don't know. But not now. What I want to know now is what happened between you and Charles. What hurt you so much?"

"He didn't know I was related to Catherine. I...purposely hid it from him. Once he learned the truth he wanted nothing more to do with me."

Kate frowned. "Then the man's a fool."

Lanni grinned, and it felt good to smile again. "If I ever see him, which is doubtful, I'll tell him you said so."

Kate's features relaxed. "Do you want to talk about him?"

Surprisingly Lanni discovered she did. She told her mother about the instant attraction she'd felt toward him, the bond they seemed to share. She described what had happened between them at the wedding ceremony. And afterward, when Charles had learned the painful truth about her family.

The wetness on her face surprised Lanni. She hadn't realized she was crying. Her mother's hand gripped hers tightly. "I'm so sorry, sweetheart. I'd give anything to have spared you this."

"But you know, Mom, the funny part is I don't regret loving Charles. Someday I'll be able to look back and realize how knowing him, loving him, changed my life. Right now it's still too new, too painful, to see what good could possibly come of all this. It's difficult, but I'm trusting that we were never meant to be together—just the way his father and Grammy were never meant to marry."

Kate wiped a tear from her own eye. "You astonish me," her mother said softly. "When did you grow up to be so wise?"

Lanni laughed and dabbed at her eyes with the napkin. "I don't feel wise at all—the only thing I feel is empty."

"That will change," Kate assured her.

Lanni knew that a time of peace and acceptance would come, but it would still take a while.

All at once her mother's face grew thoughtful. "Speaking of Charles O'Halloran, I seem to remember Matt saying something about him recently."

"Matt wants the O'Hallorans to sell him the lodge in Hard Luck," Lanni explained. She'd had several additional conversations with her brother regarding the purchase of the lodge.

"Your brother's on another one of his kicks again, isn't he?" Kate gave an exaggerated sigh.

Lanni laughed and rolled her eyes. "But this time it might be different," she said, growing serious. "I think he could do a great job with this."

"Remember when he went to cooking school?"

"How can I forget it?" Lanni asked, smiling. Matt had hoped to make his fortune with the most absurd assortment of recipes—all of which he insisted his family sample. Somehow his concoctions, teriyaki moose being his favorite, just hadn't made the splash he'd expected.

"He was a fisherman for a while, too," her mother reminded her.

"Was that before or after he decided to be an accountant? You know, Mom, maybe—just maybe—he'll be able to pull this off. He *is* serious about wanting the lodge."

"I only wish he'd done something earlier, before..."

Kate left the rest unsaid, but Lanni knew what her mother was thinking. If Matt had thought of buying the lodge sooner, he might have been able to save his marriage.

"I'm meeting him for dinner tomorrow evening," Lanni mentioned. "I'll try to find out how his plans for the lodge are progressing." The real trick, she mused, would be to find out what she could about Charles without being obvious.

No, she decided abruptly, she wouldn't ask. Charles was part of her past. He was someone she would always love, yes, but she wasn't going to look back.

CHARLES STOOD outside Matt Caldwell's apartment building. He wasn't entirely sure why this meeting was necessary. Matt had phoned and said there were papers they needed to review; since Charles was already in town, he couldn't think of a reason to refuse.

It didn't surprise him to discover he liked Matt. Under different circumstances he would have enjoyed calling Lanni's older brother his friend. Selling the lodge to a member of Catherine's family was more than a gesture of goodwill. It was his own subtle way of telling Lanni he would always love her.

Convincing Sawyer and Christian to go along with him hadn't been nearly as difficult as he'd assumed. Both his brothers were relieved that someone was going to do something about the lodge their father had built. Neither of them were interested themselves, but it seemed a shame to tear it down. They'd set a reasonable price, with excellent terms.

He checked the slip of paper for the apartment number and walked into the low-rise building. After locating the apartment, he rang the doorbell and waited.

Lanni answered.

Charles felt as if the wind had been knocked out of him.

Speechless, they stared at each other.

Shock rounded her eyes, and he noticed the way her fingers tightened around the doorknob. "Charles."

"Lanni." He'd forgotten how musical her voice was, soft and melodic. Stupidly, he looked down at the slip of paper, staring at the apartment number.

She stepped aside, obviously realizing she was blocking the door. "Come in, please."

It was all he could do to tear his gaze away from her. She was thinner and a bit pale, but he'd never seen a more beautiful woman in his life.

"Is Matt here?" he asked.

"Matt?" Once again her eyes betrayed her surprise.

"He gave me this address. Apparently there were some papers having to do with the sale of the lodge that he wanted me to read over."

"I see." She closed her eyes.

"What is it?" he asked.

"It seems we've both been tricked." She sank onto the couch as if she hadn't the strength to continue standing. "This is my place. Matt was supposed to pick me up for dinner."

"Perhaps he intended to meet us both."

"Perhaps," she agreed uncertainly. "If you'll wait here, I'll give him a call." She left momentarily and returned paler than before.

"I apologize, Charles. My brother left a message on his answering machine. He purposely arranged for the two of us to meet this evening," she said, her voice trembling. "He sent you here on a wild-goose chase and then made certain I'd be home when you arrived."

"I see." Charles wasn't sorry, but he didn't tell her that. Lanni had haunted him from the moment she'd left Hard Luck. He couldn't sleep or eat or think for want of her. No other woman had ever affected him this way.

"How are you?" he asked, his voice uncharacteristically gruff.

"Fine," she said softly, "and you?"

He sat on the chair across from her. "Fine. Sawyer and Abbey are back from their honeymoon, and Pearl Inman's getting ready to move in with her daughter."

She lowered her gaze to her hands. "I understand Matt's negotiations with you are going well."

Charles shrugged. "The fact that he's taking over the lodge helps us all." He couldn't very well admit that Lanni was the real reason he'd agreed to go ahead with the sale.

"How's Ben?" she asked.

"Cantankerous as ever."

Lanni smiled, and the knots inside him twisted to pain-inducing proportions.

"How's the new secretary doing?"

"Mariah Douglas?" Charles's smile was involuntary. "I don't think she's had much office experience. The last I heard, Christian had to show her how to change the paper in the photocopier."

"But she's stayed."

Charles nodded. "She seems determined to make a go of it. She insists on living in one of the old cabins, without electricity, because she wants those twenty acres my brothers promised her."

"Good for Mariah."

The silence stretched between them, but for some reason, it didn't bother him.

"How do you like Anchorage?" she asked.

Charles hoped she was looking for ways to continue the conversation, because he didn't want to leave, but he had no excuse to stay. "Anchorage? As far as I'm concerned it's about half an hour away from Alaska."

Lanni smiled and stared down at her hands, which were clenched tightly in her lap.

Charles had never found another woman he felt as comfortable with as Lanni. The conversation had been a little awkward at first, but once they'd both relaxed, it flowed smoothly. Had it been like this with his father and Catherine? Had his father found his soulmate in one woman while married to another?

For Lanni was his soulmate. Charles had realized that with complete certainty after she left Hard Luck. The loneliness had closed in around him. Until he'd met her, Charles had preferred his own company; in the past few weeks it felt as if a part of him was missing.

Countless times he reviewed their situation. But he'd seen the flash of pain in Ellen's eyes when she realized Lanni was related to Catherine. Charles couldn't bear to inflict that pain on Ellen again. Not when she was happy for perhaps the first time in her life.

Charles told himself to leave, but he couldn't seem to stand up and walk away.

"I have coffee on," she said. "Would you like a cup?" Her dark, luminous eyes were pleading.

He shouldn't stay. Every minute he lingered made it more difficult to go. "All right," he said, finding himself agreeing before he could change his mind.

He followed her into the kitchen. When she opened the cupboard to reach for a mug, his hand on her forearm stopped her.

"It isn't coffee I want," he told her. His eyes boldly met hers.

Her lips parted, and warm color blossomed in her cheeks. "I...I don't think this is a good idea—not for us. I—"

He cut off her words by lowering his head and kissing her. His mouth worked over hers, and as she responded, he wondered how he'd managed to last this long without her. When he ended the kiss, they were both breathing heavily. He ran his lips down the curve of her cheek to her ear.

Then he slid his mouth back to hers, and his kiss was filled with desperation. He couldn't seem to get enough of her. This was dangerous—to them both. Dragging his mouth away, he struggled for control.

Lanni buried her face in his shoulder.

"Charles..." she gasped.

"I know. I know." He was equally shaken. "It frightens me how much I want to make love to you." He was desperate for a solution, but every time he closed his eyes, all he could see was the pain on his mother's face when she realized Lanni's connection to Catherine.

"Let me love you," he whispered.

Her body tensed and she shook her head.

The rejection tore at his heart. He might not know a lot about a woman's needs and wants, but he'd have staked his life on the fact that she wanted him too.

He caught her hand and flattened it against his heart. "You want me, don't you?"

"Yes, but..." At least she was honest enough not to deny it.

"I've been half-crazy these last few weeks without you." Charles nuzzled her throat, then drew her into a lengthy, soul-shattering kiss. When he finished, she buried her face against his shoulder once more. Her body shuddered.

He kissed her again. Gently. Lips meeting lips. The mere act of touching her set his heart racing. He felt as though he were on fire. Lanni filled him with a tenderness he didn't recognize.

He wove his fingers through her long blond hair and held her protectively close.

She hung her head. "We can't go on like this."

He didn't answer, but his heart pounded wildly.

"Will our being together change anything?" she asked, her voice low and trembling. "Will I stop being Catherine Fletcher's granddaughter? Will you stop being David and Ellen's son?"

He ran his hand over his face. He had no argument to give her, no answer to make things right.

All he knew was how badly he needed her. Emotionally. Physically. And in every way you could need someone. Taking a deep breath, he shoved his fingers through his hair. "Lanni, please..."

She moved away and brushed the tumble of hair from her face in the habitual gesture he loved.

He shut his eyes and slowly lowered his head.

"Tell me, Charles. Would you have sought me out if Matt hadn't tricked us into this meeting?"

It would have been easy to lie, but he wouldn't do that. Not to Lanni. "No."

She flinched. "I didn't plan on seeing you again, either."

"But we have met," he argued, "and it's obvious we still feel the same way about each other."

"I'll always love you, Charles, but I refuse to live like this, sneaking around—"

"If we're in love, then—"

"I can't. I'm afraid...terribly afraid that history will repeat itself. My grandmother loved your father—and she was never more than his mistress—a small part of his life. I can't live like that."

"I'd never ask that of you. *I'm* not married to someone else!"

"But you'll always feel torn," she said. "You love me, but you love your family, too, and so you should. But your mother could never accept me."

He didn't reply.

"I apologize for what Matt did. I'll make sure it doesn't happen again," she whispered brokenly, moving into the living room and gesturing at the door. "Perhaps it would be better if you left now."

Charles reached the door and stopped, his back toward her. "I can't go," he said. "I can't leave you like this." He wasn't sure what his staying would accomplish; it might do more harm than good. One thing was certain—he couldn't right the sins of generations past.

He blindly made his way back into the kitchen. He might not have wanted coffee earlier, but he felt a desperate need for something now.

By the time he found the mugs, Lanni had joined him.

"Do you want some?" he asked.

"Please."

He poured them each a cup and carried them to the small table. Lanni gave him a weak smile as they sat facing each other. Knowing he was the one responsible for the shadows under her eyes damn near broke his heart.

"I . . . I want to thank you," she said.

"Thank me?" He'd done nothing but bring pain into her life, just as his father had brought pain to her grandmother.

"For what you've done to help my brother."

The time for pretense was gone. "I sold the lodge for a number of reasons, not all of them noble."

"I don't understand."

"I'm not sure I do, either." The coffee tasted slightly burned and bitter. That seemed fitting somehow. "I suppose I thought that if your brother managed the lodge, I had a way of learning about you. Not that I intended to pry into your private life."

"I see."

"I figured your brother would let me know when you got married..." His heart clenched at the thought of Lanni with another man. "I'm sorry for what happened this evening. I never meant to hurt you." His words were jagged. He took a hurried drink of the coffee to cover how difficult it had been to say them.

Tears glistened in her eyes. "Some things were never meant to be."

He stood up to carry the mug to the sink. He looked back at her and resisted the urge to bid her farewell.

They'd already said their goodbyes.

"So," MATT SAID when he phoned Lanni the following morning. "I don't suppose you had any company drop by unannounced last evening, did you?"

"Yes." Her brother didn't have any idea how much his actions had hurt her.

"Well, don't keep me in suspense. Tell me what happened."

"Why would you do such a thing?" Lanni asked, her throat burning as she struggled to keep her voice level. She knew her brother would never intentionally hurt her. Yet he might as well have driven a knife into her heart as invite Charles into her home.

"Why would I arrange for Charles and you to meet?" Matt repeated. "Because it was crystal clear to me from the moment I met O'Halloran that he's in love with you."

Lanni said nothing.

"It was also crystal clear to me that you're in love with him!"

Again she didn't bother to contradict him.

"I don't know what nonsense is keeping you apart, but I thought it was time someone did something."

"Of all the people in the world," she blurted, "I would think you'd be the one to respect another person's privacy." Lanni was close to tears. "You love Karen and—"

"What's she got to do with this?" he interjected.

"—she loves you!"

"Right. She couldn't get to that attorney fast enough to file for the divorce. In case you didn't know, that's not the action of a woman in love."

"I won't take sides, Matt. I didn't all through the divorce, and I won't now. All I know is that you love her, and I strongly suspect she still loves you. How would *you* feel if I tricked you into meeting her?"

Matt's voice hardened. "Don't ever try it, little sister."

"That's what I thought."

Suddenly he chuckled as if something amused him. "Karen and I would probably end up killing each other. Now that she's moved, I can see the wisdom of having her gone."

"Wisdom?"

"I don't have to worry about seeing her with another man, do I?"

"No."

They both hesitated.

"I apologize if I did the wrong thing," Matt said brusquely. "It sounds like I made the situation worse, instead of better."

"It doesn't matter."

"I'm not much of a matchmaker, am I?"

"I wouldn't know about that, but the next time I want to meet a man, you're the last person I'll ask for help."

"Why's that?"

"I don't think I could go through another evening like last night."

When Matt spoke again, he sounded uncertain. "I did read you right, didn't I? You are in love with him?"

"Yes," she said hoarsely. "But it's over—the same as you and Karen. There's nothing left to resurrect. If you have any feelings for me as your sister, you won't pull this kind of stunt again."

"I won't," Matt promised.

Lanni believed him.

At noon she went to check her mailbox. There was one letter—with a Canadian postmark. But she was almost sure she didn't know anyone living in Vancouver, British Columbia.

She waited until she was back in the apartment before opening the envelope. She pulled out a sheet of personalized stationery. The embossed letterhead said Ellen Greenleaf.

With shaky knees, Lanni pulled out a kitchen chair and sat down to read.

Dear Lanni,

I imagine this letter comes as a surprise. Sawyer was kind enough to obtain your address for me. I've debated for several weeks now on how to contact you, and decided the best way was by letter.

First, I want to apologize for my behavior at Sawyer and Abbey's wedding. Discovering you're a relative of Catherine Fletcher's came as a shock. I fear I was far less gracious than I should have been. I beg your forgiveness for anything I might have said or done to hurt you.

I can't be certain what you do or don't know about my relationship with Catherine—or more importantly, my late husband's relationship with her. As far as I'm concerned, all that was laid to rest with David. I harbor Catherine no ill will. Nor you.

Before Charles learned of your tie with Catherine, he confided in me his feelings for you. It is my understanding that you have since returned to Anchorage. I tried to ask Charles about the two of you, but he refuses to discuss the matter.

However, I know my son. I've attempted to convince him, without success, that you shouldn't be blamed for the sins of another.

It breaks my heart to think that another generation is about to suffer because of me. I find that I'll be in Anchorage next week. Would it be possible for us to have lunch? I'll be staying at the Alaska Inn. If you could give me a call on Tuesday morning, perhaps we could schedule lunch.

It's time we buried the past.

Most Sincerely,
Ellen Greenleaf

CHAPTER NINE

SAWYER WAS PORING over a cookbook when Abbey walked in the front door. She stopped a minute, amused at what a discordant sight her husband made with a lace-fringed apron tied around his waist.

"Hi, honey, I'm home," she called, slipping off her shoes.

"Thank goodness." Sawyer stripped off the apron and tossed it aside. "I can't even begin to figure out these instructions."

"What did you decide to cook?"

"Chicken cordon bleu."

"Cordon bleu? When you said you'd fix dinner, I assumed you'd pick something easy."

"This looked easy enough," he said, peering down at the photograph accompanying the recipe. "We've got the chicken, the cheese and just about everything else I need except the patience."

Abbey wrapped her arms around him and smiled into his face. "You want me to come to the rescue, do you?"

He kissed her. "Please."

"It's going to cost you," she teased.

"I'll pay—price is no object."

Abbey reached for the cookbook while Sawyer tied the apron around her.

"Well?" he asked when she'd finished reading the recipe.

"I'll do what I can," she said, feigning uncertainty. "But I'm not promising anything."

Sawyer poured himself a cup of coffee and sat down to watch her. Abbey efficiently assembled ingredients from the cupboard and the refrigerator. After a few minutes, he said, "Charles is back."

"Oh," Abbey said absently. "Has his mood improved?"

"No. If anything it's worse. I don't think I've ever seen him more miserable."

Abbey looked up, concerned. "Have you tried talking to him?"

"Twice now, and both times he nearly bit my head off. You can take my word for it, he isn't in a communicative mood."

"It's Lanni, isn't it?"

Sawyer frowned. "That's my guess."

"Maybe I should try talking to him." She studied her husband.

"I wouldn't advise it," Sawyer murmured. "Charles will work this out in his own time and his own way. He's struggling with the fact that he loves Lanni. My brother never expected to fall in love."

"You didn't, either," Abbey reminded him.

"That's true," Sawyer said with a wide grin. "As you recall I had some trouble getting used to the idea myself." More seriously he said, "It's even harder for Charles, because he didn't fall in love with just anyone. Nope, that would've been too easy. He had to go and fall for Catherine Fletcher's granddaughter. So he's making all kinds of excuses why a relationship between them won't work."

"How do you mean?"

"Lanni's nearly ten years younger, so out of the blue, Charles announces she's too young to know what she wants. Then he mumbled something about Lanni and some newspaper." He shook his head. "I haven't got a clue what he was talking about there."

"Lanni shouldn't be blamed for the sins of her grandmother."

"I don't think Charles blames her. I suspect he feels he's being disloyal to our mother. You have to understand, Catherine did everything in her power to destroy my family."

Abbey sat down across the table from her husband. "It seems such a pity the way everything's turned out between Charles and Lanni. They really care about each other."

"Being in love doesn't automatically make everything right," Sawyer said.

"No, it doesn't," Abbey agreed, "but it's a step in that direction."

Sawyer's hand gripped hers, and he raised her knuckles to his lips. "I sure hope so."

Scott burst into the kitchen just then, Eagle Catcher at his heels. The boy's face was red and sweaty with exertion; her son always went at full speed, Abbey thought, her heart filled with tenderness.

"What's for dinner?" Scott asked. "I'm starved."

He looked at Sawyer, who'd made a grandiose announcement that morning about cooking a special meal. Flustered, Sawyer shrugged.

"Chicken with cheese and rice," Abbey answered.

Scott beamed with approval. "Sounds good."

"It's an old family recipe," Sawyer assured him. "Handed down from generation to generation."

"I bet I'll like it, then."

"I bet you will, too," Sawyer said and winked at his wife.

LANNI WALKED into the formal dining room of the Alaska Inn and looked quickly around. She was meeting Charles's mother here. The room's opulent decor was reminiscent of the Roaring Twenties, Alaska style, with red velvet wallpaper, a rich-looking red carpet and red velvet cushions on the chairs.

Lanni saw Ellen Greenleaf almost right away. The dignified woman sat at a table next to the window, apparently deep in thought, for she didn't seem to notice Lanni's approach.

"Mrs. Greenleaf," Lanni said gently, not wanting to startle the woman.

"Lanni," Ellen said, smiling in welcome. "Please, sit down."

Lanni pulled out the chair and sat down across from Ellen. She took a nervous moment to tuck her purse between her feet and place her napkin on her lap.

"It's good of you to meet me," Ellen began.

"Oh, no, it's my pleasure," Lanni said. "I appreciated your letter more than I can say. And please, you don't need to worry about what happened at Sawyer's wedding."

The waiter appeared and they both ordered quickly, getting that out of the way. Lanni's mind wasn't on food; she felt much too flustered to think about eating.

"How are you?" Charles's mother asked first.

Lanni didn't know if there was some hidden meaning in the question. "Uh, fine, thank you. And you?"

Ellen nodded. "I don't mean to hedge with small talk. It's just that I find what I'm about to tell you very...difficult. You see, it happened so many years ago

I wonder if exhuming the past will do either of us any good."

Lanni sipped from her ice water, concentrating on the coldness of the glass. She'd noticed how drawn and pale Ellen looked. "I don't want you to say or do anything that makes you uncomfortable."

Ellen seemed not to have heard. "I remember your mother so very well. Kate was a delightful little girl, with bright eyes and long, thick braids. I used to see her when she visited her mother during the summer. I desperately longed for a child myself, and Catherine never lost an opportunity to taunt me."

Lanni lowered her gaze. "I'm sorry."

"No, I apologize," Ellen said, and sighed. "I didn't ask you to lunch to discuss your grandmother's faults. Actually I've come to confess my own."

Lanni grew more troubled. It was obvious that Ellen felt unsure about this conversation. She'd instigated their meeting, yet seemed to question the wisdom of it.

"From what I understand, there are grievances on both sides," Lanni said.

Ellen's nod was almost imperceptible. "That's true enough. Truer than you'll ever know."

"My grandmother isn't well these days."

"I'm sorry to hear it," Ellen murmured. "I'm sincere about that, whether you choose to believe me or not."

"I do believe you."

Ellen lifted the water glass to her lips; when she set it back down on the table, she appeared to be readying herself for some sort of ordeal. She straightened her back, and Lanni noticed the way she repeatedly clenched and unclenched her hands.

"I find it somewhat...ironic that you're the one I'm telling this to. My sons know nothing of what I'm about to explain. I've kept this secret locked in my heart for nearly fifty years."

Lanni was amazed herself. She was almost a stranger to Ellen Greenleaf; more than that, she was the grand-daughter of Ellen's oldest enemy. Yet Charles's mother had chosen to confide in her.

"Mrs. Greenleaf—"

"Please, call me Ellen."

"Ellen, I think—"

It was as if Ellen hadn't heard her. "In all fairness, I've decided Charles should be told the facts, as well. I'll leave the decision to tell Sawyer and Christian up to Charles."

Lanni didn't know what to say. She didn't want to mislead Ellen into thinking she had a relationship with Charles when she didn't. "I don't—it isn't likely I'll see Charles again."

"I sincerely hope that isn't the case." Ellen sighed again and gazed into the distance. "My son will live his own life, make his own decisions and live by them. What he does or doesn't do with this information is en-tirely up to him. The same way it will be up to you."

"Ellen, I'm not sure you should tell me...whatever this is."

The older woman shook her head. "I feel otherwise, and I'll explain later."

Lanni might have argued further, but their food ar-rived. Neither seemed to have any interest in eating. Lanni reached for her fork and ate a couple of shrimp, then contented herself with pushing the lettuce leaves about her plate.

Ellen moved her salad aside and picked up her water glass again. Then she began to speak. "It all started in the last days of World War II. I lost my parents in a London bombing. My older brother was a bombardier. His plane went down over Germany in June of 1943. Other than one older cousin, Elizabeth, I had no family left."

Lanni's heart constricted; she was close to her own family and losing them seemed unimaginable. "How alone you must have felt."

"I did. I was lost and lonely and desperately afraid. That was when I met a young American soldier."

David was lonely, too, Lanni realized. So far from home, enduring the shock and horror of war, devastated by the death of his brother.

"We fell in love. I've never loved as deeply or as completely in my life. We clung to each other, and the love we shared was the only thing that kept me sane in those last terrible months of the war." Ellen paused, her eyes glistening with tears. It took several moments for her to compose herself.

"Perhaps we should continue sometime later," Lanni suggested.

"No. The telling won't be any easier. I've come this far... I don't know if I'll have the courage to continue later."

Lanni reached across the table and gripped Ellen's hand.

"I was raised in a God-fearing home," Ellen said in a low voice. "I'm not offering any excuses for what happened, but you have to understand how desperate the times were. I was deeply in love, and I didn't know from one day to the next what the future held. My family had been wiped out. He was so far from home.

It seemed inevitable that we give in to our natural inclinations and make love."

Lanni recalled how close she and Charles had come to surrendering themselves. "I would never judge you, Ellen."

Charles's mother smiled softly, sadly. "We lived for those few tender moments together. With each other, we found a confirmation of life, a solace that had escaped us."

She hesitated, and Lanni remained silent, not wanting to interrupt Ellen's painfully remembered—and painfully told—story with questions.

"The inevitable happened. We were careless, and I soon discovered I was pregnant."

"Pregnant?" Lanni repeated, blinking back her surprise.

Ellen nodded. "I was so afraid to tell him. So embarrassed that I'd been this foolish. I avoided him, but he found me and confronted me. I was sure he wouldn't want me anymore, but when I told him about the baby, he was ecstatic." Her eyes grew warm with the memory. "He lifted me off the ground and and kissed me until I was senseless. Because he was happy, I was, too." A smile brightened her pale features. "We planned to marry as quickly as possible. He... he was making the arrangements when... when he was sent on a mission." She paused and seemed to gather herself together.

"You see he... he never returned. I didn't learn until two agonizing weeks later that he'd been killed."

Lanni frowned. "David killed?"

"No. The father of my child was Charles O'Halloran. David's brother."

Lanni was left speechless. She started to ask the most obvious questions but found that her throat had closed up.

"I think . . . no, I know I would have died had it not been for David and the baby. Losing my brother and my parents broke my heart. Losing Charles crushed my spirit. I had no will to continue."

"Did you ever find out what happened to Charles?"

Ellen slowly shook her head. "No one will ever really know. The only thing I'm confident of is that he loved me and he wanted our child."

"So David found you?"

"Yes. Charles and his brother were very close. As I look back on that time, I think Charles might have known on some level that he wouldn't make it back. David told me his brother had come to him and asked him to take care of me if anything happened. David gave his brother his word of honor that he would."

Lanni closed her eyes.

"At first all he intended to do was arrange for me to join his family in Alaska."

"And he couldn't," Lanni guessed.

"The only way it turned out to be possible was if he married me himself. I should never have agreed. Over the years I regretted it thousands of times. In my own defense, though, I was in a haze of pain and grief. The pregnancy wasn't going well, and the thought of being alone terrified me."

"You did eventually come to love him."

"Oh, yes, eventually." Ellen's eyes took on that faraway look again. "When I married him, I didn't know about Catherine. David never mentioned her, and if Charles had ever told me about his brother's fiancée, I'd forgotten."

"What about the baby?"

"Two months after the wedding—when I was six months pregnant—I gave birth to a daughter. She lived two days... We buried her in London. I named her Emily after the sister my Charles lost. I thought he would approve."

"I'm sure he would have." Lanni felt the tears gathering, and her heart went out to Charles's mother. She'd lost her family, the father of her child and then her child.

"David was so gentle with me. We wept together, and he stood by my side when we buried Emily. I wanted to release him from the wedding vows, but he refused. Soon afterward, he was given his orders to return home. We returned together."

"That was when you found out about Catherine?"

"Yes," Ellen answered softly. "In the beginning I was upset that David hadn't mentioned her. But he insisted he'd made the decision to marry me and he wanted me as his wife. You see, by that time we'd become lovers, although I don't believe we were in love. Not then. I'm ashamed to admit that in the beginning when David made love to me I pretended it was Charles. I prayed he never knew, but I strongly suspect he did."

"You waited almost fifteen years to start a family."

Ellen shook her head. "It wasn't our choice. There never seemed to be any medical reason I couldn't conceive. I had easily enough before. Both David and I went through numerous tests and the doctors always came up blank." She gave a deep sigh. "In retrospect I realize I needed those years to heal emotionally from the war. It wasn't until I was in my midthirties that I became pregnant with Charles."

Named after the brother who'd died. The lover who'd never returned.

"In many ways the two Charleses are alike," Ellen said on a wistful note. "I've marveled over the years at the similarities between them. Sawyer, on the other hand, is a lot like his father in looks and temperament."

"Christian must take after your side of the family, then" Lanni commented. "In appearance, anyway." The youngest O'Halloran brother's hair color was much lighter than that of his siblings.

Ellen answered her with a nod. "I wished desperately for a daughter, but it was never meant to be."

"You and David separated for a time, didn't you?"

"Yes. We'd been married close to thirty years by then. Charles was fifteen at the time, Sawyer a couple of years younger." Ellen hesitated as if she wasn't sure she should continue. "I'd been back to England only once in all those years. I'd never done well in Alaska. I realize now that part of this was my own fault, but part was due to... other factors."

Lanni had the feeling some of those factors had to do with Catherine.

"I missed England. I'd always missed England. My cousin, Elizabeth, wrote and urged me to visit. David and I argued, which was something we frequently did in those days. He didn't want me to leave.

"In all the years we'd lived together, not once had he ever said he regretted marrying me. He did that day, in anger. That was when I realized how much my weakness had hurt him.

"I'm not proud of what happened next. In my outrage I told him I'd never loved him. It was a lie. A woman can't live with a man, bear his children and feel nothing. I'd grown to love David as much as it was possible to love anyone, but I was afraid to tell him that.

"The next morning I packed my bags and left for England with Christian."

"David didn't come after you?"

"No. His pride wouldn't allow that."

"How sad for you both."

"It was a very painful time," Ellen acknowledged simply. "I returned to England, the home and country I'd yearned for all those years, and discovered I no longer belonged. Christian was miserable, too. Pride carried me through the first year, but the months that followed were . . . difficult."

"You were in touch with David?"

"Oh, yes. I had to keep in touch because of the boys. I missed them terribly and they missed me. I'd thought that with Charles and Sawyer in their teen years, my presence wouldn't be that important or necessary to them. I was wrong."

"What brought you home?"

Ellen smiled softly. "I admitted to David that I'd lied. I did love him, and had for many years. I asked him to forgive me for being so foolish. He said he was sorry, too. I told him I wanted to come home."

"And you were happy afterward?"

"Yes," she said, but her eyes revealed how short-lived that happiness was. "In the beginning we were. It was as if we'd both been given a fresh start. I tried in every way I knew to show David how important he was to me.

"He was a gentle, noble man who'd sacrificed a great deal to fulfill a promise to his brother. For the first time since we married he wanted me, and not because of any obligation. Or so I believed."

"That was when my grandmother destroyed your marriage, wasn't it?"

"No," Ellen surprised her by saying.

"David and I did that on our own. Certainly she contributed to the problem, but I can't blame her for David's or my stubbornness. When I learned about their affair, I was deeply hurt. David had had the perfect opportunity to suggest a divorce. Instead, he'd invited me home. I came back because I thought he wanted me...."

"Why *did* he ask you to come back?"

"I don't think I'll ever fully understand his reasons. I'd like to believe he was sincere about wanting our marriage to work. For the boys' sake, yes, but for us, as well. England wasn't the homeland I'd left—almost against my will Alaska had become my home.

"When I learned about the affair, I moved out of David's bedroom and asked for a divorce. David wouldn't hear of it. That was when he built the lodge.

"I always hated that place, while David became more and more obsessed with it. Soon we were like strangers. We rarely spoke to each other. I fully expected him to leave me for Catherine, and I never understood why he didn't. To the best of my knowledge he never slept with her again after I returned from England, but I can't be sure."

"She waited for him," Lanni whispered. "She waited for the marriage to end so she'd be free to take him for herself."

"I lived with that knowledge every day of our marriage."

"My grandmother is a bitter, unhappy woman."

Ellen shook her head slowly. "I'm afraid she has been from the day I stepped out of the plane with David and he introduced me as his wife."

Ellen didn't blame Catherine for ruining her marriage, and by the same token Catherine had to take responsibility for what she'd made of her own life.

"I'm still not sure I understand why you've told me all this," Lanni said. Her salad remained almost untouched, as did Ellen's.

"My son loves you."

"I love him."

"Then go to him, Lanni. Fight for him. Don't allow the mistakes I made, the sins both your grandmother and I committed, to influence your life. Marry Charles, with my blessing. Make him happy and, if you're both willing, make me a grandmother."

Lanni's eyes held Ellen's. "I'll do what I can," she said decisively, "but Charles is a stubborn man."

"Be even more stubborn, then," she advised. "I lost my Charles, not by choice, but by fate. Don't lose yours."

Lanni's eyes gleamed with determination. "I won't. Not now."

Ellen laughed gently. "You know, I almost feel sorry for the boy."

Before she was through with him, Lanni decided, Charles might well be in need of his mother's sympathy.

"I SUPPOSE you heard," Ben told Charles when he walked into the Hard Luck Café.

"Heard what?"

"About Pete and Dotty. They've announced their engagement."

Charles slid onto a stood without comment. Feeling the way he had lately, he found it difficult to dredge up enthusiasm for much of anything. If Pete Livengood was marrying the nurse Christian had hired, then great. Wonderful.

"Aren't you going to say something?" Ben asked, pouring him a cup of coffee.

"Yeah, more power to them both."

"The wedding's in two months."

The last thing Charles wanted to discuss was weddings.

Ben lingered at the counter. "Rumor has it you're selling the lodge."

"Yeah," he answered without elaborating.

"When did this all happen?"

"Last week."

"Well, who bought it? Anyone I know?" Ben was beginning to sound decidedly short-tempered.

"I doubt it."

"Listen, Charles, if talking with a friend is too much trouble for you, just say the word and I'll shut my trap."

Charles scowled. "I came in for coffee, not conversation."

"Fine." Ben set down the pot so hard coffee splashed on the counter. Then he marched back into the kitchen, where he slammed dishes and pans around with more noise than Charles suspected was necessary.

Listening to the racket, he regretted his own outburst. Ben was a damn good friend and deserved better.

"Matt Caldwell bought the lodge," he said when Ben reappeared.

The older man ignored him.

"Matt is Lanni's brother."

Still Ben went about his business as if he was alone in the café.

The door opened and Mitch Harris stepped inside. He slipped onto a stool two down from Charles. The two men acknowledged each other with a brief nod of the head. Mitch hadn't been in Hard Luck all that long, but Charles liked him. Liked his understated authority, his kindness—and the fact that Mitch, too, was a man of few words.

Ben took Mitch's order and continued to ignore Charles.

"All right," Charles snapped when his friend paraded past yet again. "If you're looking for an apology, you've got one."

To his amazement Ben whirled about and grinned broadly. "You know what your problem is, don't you?"

As a matter of fact, Charles did. His problem, as Ben referred to it, was about five foot six with long blond hair and eyes that could look straight through his soul.

Ben didn't give him a chance to respond. "In case no one's bothered to tell you, you've got a chip on your shoulder the size of this great state of ours."

"Thank you, I appreciate hearing that," Charles muttered sarcastically.

"Now if you want to make a mess of your life, that's your business. I told you what I thought. Most of the others share my opinion, but they don't have the guts to tell you. You seem to—"

"I saw Lanni while I was in Anchorage," Charles broke in, his voice low. He paused; he wasn't sure why he felt it was necessary for Ben to know that.

However, his comment had piqued Ben's interest. "You did?"

Charles stared into his coffee mug. "Her brother tricked us into a meeting. We both realize a relationship between us isn't meant to be. She feels as strongly about it as I do." Even now, Charles didn't understand why he'd stayed in her apartment once he knew what Matt had done. Any man with a lick of sense would have known better. The only thing he'd managed to prove was how much he loved her.

Instinctively he recognized that true satisfaction would escape him with another woman. Any other woman. He would find what he needed only with Lanni.

The door opened, and Christian entered the café, frowning. "Got anything stronger than coffee?" he asked Ben.

"You know I only sell beer on Friday and Saturday nights."

"I was hoping you'd make an exception this afternoon."

"What's up?" Charles asked.

Christian regarded him wanly. "Have you rejoined the living, or are you still a brooding, bad-tempered zombie?"

"I'm still brooding and bad-tempered, but that doesn't mean you can't answer the question."

"Mariah Douglas."

"Who?"

"The new secretary," Ben supplied.

"The woman's incompetent," Christian snapped.

"Then fire her," Charles suggested.

"I've tried. Three times to be exact, and then she bursts into tears and tells me how terribly sorry she is, and before I know it she's talked me into giving her another chance.''

"Is Sawyer having the same kind of problems with her?" Charles wanted to know. It seemed to him that his brother wouldn't have any qualms about laying off an inept employee.

"That's what's so screwy. I swear if Sawyer asks Mariah to type anything, she goes at it about a hundred miles an hour and produces a flawless copy."

"But not for you?"

"For me she spills coffee over the keyboard. For me she topples a hundred-pound filing cabinet onto my foot. For me she cuts off a phone call to an important client.''

"I'd say you have a negative effect on the woman."

Christian rested his elbows on the counter and dropped his head into his hands. "I don't know what to do anymore."

"Is she still living in the cabin?" Ben asked.

"Oh, yes. I don't know what possessed me to actually think a woman from the big city, accustomed to modern conveniences, could live out there. But Mariah refuses to listen to reason. For the life of me, I can't convince her to move.''

Charles found himself enjoying the fact that his youngest brother was experiencing women troubles. He obviously hadn't managed to conceal his reaction from Christian.

Christian raised his head and looked at Charles through narrowed eyes. "If I were you I wouldn't look so damn smug."

"Why's that?" Charles had to admit it felt good to smile.

"You know Matt Caldwell's in town?"

"Already?" Ben said. "The man isn't going to let any grass grow under his feet, is he?"

The two brothers ignored him. Charles said, "I understand he's bringing in supplies. What he said to me in Anchorage is that he wants to get as much done on the lodge as possible before the weather changes."

"Supplies aren't the only thing he brought with him," Christian muttered.

Charles frowned. "What do you mean?"

"Nothing," his brother said abruptly, and slid off the stool. He set a dollar bill and some change down on the counter, then gave a jaunty little wave. "Thanks for the coffee, Ben. I'll be back Friday night when you can serve me something more to my liking."

Charles knew that Matt had flown in on the morning flight. One of the air services out of Fairbanks had brought him, along with enough building supplies to keep him busy the entire winter.

He'd need at least that much time. While part of the structure hadn't been seriously damaged by the flames, much of it was in bad shape. Matt would have to work fast if he intended to live in the lodge this year. Winter arrived early in Hard Luck; it wasn't uncommon for the rivers to freeze over in September.

Wondering about Christian's cryptic remark, Charles got up from the counter and strolled outside. He hadn't exactly intended to become close friends with Matt Caldwell, but the least he could do was stop by to say hello and see if there was anything he needed.

Knowing his new sister-in-law, he figured Abbey had probably invited Matt to dinner. She and Sawyer would provide a hearty welcome to their community's newest member. He smiled when he thought of the changes in Sawyer since he'd met Abbey.

When Charles arrived at the lodge, he heard a volley of hammering. The sound of voices followed. Charles hadn't realized Matt had brought anyone with him; actually he'd been smart to do so. With everything that needed to be done before the weather became prohibitive, getting the lodge in shape would take more than one pair of hands.

It felt strange to knock at the front door of a place he'd once considered his own. Almost immediately, Matt was there, greeting him warmly. "Charles! Come in. Uh, I take it you heard."

"Heard what?"

"It's Charles," he shouted over his shoulder. "And I don't think it's me he's come to see." Matt's deep brown eyes sparkled with mischief.

"Is something going on here that I don't know about?"

"Hello, Charles." Lanni stepped out from one of the back rooms. She wore jeans and carried a hammer, which she swung idly at her side. "I wondered how long it would take you to discover I'd moved to Hard Luck."

CHAPTER TEN

"WHAT DO YOU MEAN you've moved to Hard Luck?" Charles demanded. He scowled at her, but his lack of enthusiasm didn't appear to discourage her.

The hammer continued to swing at her side, and she wore a sassy grin. "What do you think I mean?"

That she intended to make his life a living hell, Charles decided. "What about the job with the newspaper?"

She shrugged, as if it was of no importance. Charles knew otherwise. Matt had bragged to him about Lanni's talents. Being accepted as an intern at the Anchorage daily paper was no small feat. If he remembered correctly, Lanni was scheduled to begin work the first week of September. It was the chance of a lifetime for her, and he refused to let her walk away from the opportunity because of him. Or because of some misguided belief that they could work things out.

"Damn it, Lanni, you were supposed to be working for the newspaper in another two weeks."

The saucy look she wore began to waver. "I guess I won't be, after all."

"Why the hell not?"

"Lanni," Matt called out. He stuck his head around the corner and saw the two of them talking. A grin spread across his face. "Never mind," he said, looking pleased with himself.

"Answer my question!" Charles glared at her.

"If you must know," she said stiffly, "I've turned the job down."

"You can't do that!"

"I tried to talk some sense into her," Matt insisted, peeking around the corner again, "but she refused to listen."

"Go away, Matt," Lanni said. "This conversation doesn't include you."

"Sorry." Matt stepped onto the porch and stood, feet braced wide apart like a gunslinger, thumbs tucked into his toolbelt. A hammer hung from one side like a red-hot six-shooter. "I don't think she should turn it down, either. Maybe you can talk some sense into her."

"What happens with my career is entirely up to me," Lanni answered calmly.

"Take the job!" Charles barked. The decision was simple: he didn't want her in Hard Luck. Not where she could torment him day and night. He had trouble re-sisting her when she was half a state away; he'd be in serious trouble if she moved virtually next door.

"He's right, sis."

"Matt," Lanni said in a low, angry whisper. "Let me repeat—this conversation is between Charles and me."

"All right, all right," Matt said, and held up both hands in surrender. "I'll leave." He strode sheepishly past them and out the front door, stopping to whisper something to Lanni that Charles couldn't hear.

The door closed with an ominous slam.

"Perhaps we should sit down and talk about this," Lanni suggested.

Charles stiffened, unwilling to be drawn into an argument. He felt himself weakening just being close to Lanni. Her smile cut straight through his pride and sliced away his resolve. "There's nothing to discuss."

"That's not true." Her voice was calm and controlled.

"You'll be wasting your time."

"I don't see it that way."

"I'm leaving town this afternoon," he told her sharply. That much was true—for some unknown reason his mother wanted to see him. She'd insisted on meeting him and had suggested Fairbanks. He'd agreed with reluctance, but was grateful now for the excuse.

"I'll be here waiting for you when you get back," Lanni told him.

His hands knotted into tight fists. "Lanni, no."

The tender look she gave him told Charles it would take an act of God to get her to return to Anchorage. He could disappear into the tundra for weeks on end, often did, and it wouldn't matter. Not to her. She'd still be here, waiting.

He ran his fingers through his hair. "Why are you doing this?" he asked in exasperation.

"Because I love you. We belong together. I didn't understand that until . . . recently. Your mother helped me see—"

"My mother?" He was unable to hide his surprise. "What's she got to do with this?"

Lanni's eyes widened. "You mean to say she hasn't talked to you yet?"

He didn't answer. Frankly he didn't like the idea of his mother meddling in his life.

"I've never been one to believe in fate," Lanni continued, "but now I'm not so sure. It's as if the two of us were destined for each other. In some bizarre way I was sent into your life and you into mine. And one of the reasons for this is to right a wrong done half a century ago. We didn't fall in love by accident," she said, her look intent. "You, Charles O'Halloran, are my destiny. Love me or not, I'm yours."

Charles could see that no amount of logic would help. So the only option she left him was cruelty. "I suggest you leave Hard Luck now. If you don't, you'll become just like your grandmother, wasting your life over a man she can't have."

Lanni blanched, and he noticed how she took a step back as if he'd physically threatened her. The temptation to rush to her and beg her forgiveness was nearly overpowering.

"There's something you're forgetting in all this," she said in a voice that was decidedly shaky. "David loved Catherine. You told me so yourself. Just the way you love me. Insulting me and my family isn't going to help."

It *had* to help. Insults were the only tool left in his fast-depleting arsenal.

"I refuse to believe you don't love me, Charles. You can try of course, but I don't know how you'll manage to keep up the facade when we live in the same town."

"Fine, then. We'll be lovers if that's what you want." He tried again, desperate for her to see reason. "It was all my father was willing to offer your grandmother. And it's all I'm offering you."

She hesitated, her eyes revealing her pain. The confidence she'd exuded earlier had vanished. Once again

Charles had to restrain himself from reaching for her, comforting her. He didn't know what madness had possessed her to return. There was no hope for their relationship. As far as he was concerned, the matter was settled.

She said nothing.

"What the hell do you intend to do?" he demanded. His patience hung by a fraying thread.

"Exactly what I planned from the first. I'll help Matt as long as I can."

"Then what?" he pressed.

A slow, satisfied smile curved her lips. "I came back for you, Charles O'Halloran, and I'll be waiting for you."

"YOU'VE BEEN THOUGHTFUL all evening," Abbey said to her husband.

Sawyer sat in his favorite chair, his feet propped on the matching ottoman. The Fairbanks newspaper lay unread in his lap as he stared blankly into the distance. "Something's not right," he murmured.

Abbey sat on the arm of the overstuffed chair and rested her cheek on his shoulder. "Not right with what?"

"My brother."

Abbey kissed the top of Sawyer's head. "I know you're worried about Charles again, but he's got to figure things out for himself."

"I suppose," he answered absently. Sawyer slid his arm about her waist. "I got word that Bethany Ross, one of the new schoolteachers is flying into town the first of next week."

Abbey was relieved. The kids were ready for school to start if Susan's recent chatter was anything to go by. Just that morning she'd found her playing school with Chrissie Harris. The two girls had become almost inseparable over the summer months, and Abbey was grateful her children had adjusted so readily to life in the Alaskan interior. They'd need to adapt to school here, too, but they wouldn't be the only ones. The teachers—one for elementary school to the sixth grade, the other for seventh grade through high school—were also new this year.

It amazed Abbey that there were fewer students in Hard Luck than there were teachers in the Seattle school her kids had attended the previous year. Considering the size of the community, Abbey reflected, her children had made friends very quickly in Hard Luck. Scott and Ronny Gold had discovered each other the very day they arrived. It was almost the same story with Susan and Chrissie—Mitch Harris's daughter—who spent her days with Ronny's mother, Louise.

"Charles flew into Fairbanks this afternoon. He didn't mention why he was going," Sawyer said, breaking into Abbey's thoughts.

"He doesn't need to check in with you, does he?"

"No. It's just that..."

"Just what?"

"He wasn't the same when he returned."

"Don't you think that might have something to do with Lanni moving back to town?"

"Possibly," Sawyer agreed, "but he knew she was living at the lodge before he left. Fact is, he was telling me what a damn fool she was."

Abbey hid a smile. "A fool, you say. She must be in love with an O'Halloran."

Sawyer chuckled, gripped Abbey about the waist and pulled her into his lap. "I could take offense at that."

Abbey's eyes met his and the laughter drained away. "I was only teasing. You know how much I love you."

"I know." He touched his forehead to hers. "I'm worried. About Charles."

"Don't be," Abbey told him gently. "From my admittedly limited experience, I've learned that things usually have a way of righting themselves."

"My wife, the eternal optimist." Sawyer kissed the tip of her nose.

"Don't you feel Charles and Lanni should be together?" Abbey asked. It was something she'd sensed almost from the first. Fate. Providence. Whatever you wanted to call it.

"I don't know." Sawyer shook his head. "In the beginning I was as confident as you."

"And now?"

"Now I don't know what to think. Charles is obviously miserable, not that he'll admit it. At first I blamed myself—I should have told him who Lanni's related to, and I still don't understand why I didn't. I guess I liked seeing him flustered over a woman."

"Flustered?"

"The way you flustered me from the moment we met," Sawyer said, touching his lips to hers. "Later I realized what a dirty trick I'd pulled on him, and I regretted it."

"I don't believe it would have mattered," Abbey said thoughtfully. "Lanni's being related to Catherine, I mean. He fell for her hook, line and sinker."

"The poor man was doomed."

"Doomed?" Abbey raised her eyebrows. "You might have come up with a more flattering term. I believe they were meant to be together," she said again. "Maybe the two of them are supposed to make up for the wrongs in the past."

Sawyer grinned. "In other words, my poor brother's doomed."

Abbey tickled her husband in retaliation, and then Sawyer found an even more effective revenge. It was a very long time before either of them worried about Charles or Lanni again.

LANNI SAT on the top step of the porch while her brother worked inside the lodge. Matt was reviewing his finances in an effort to calculate how long it would be before he could attract paying customers. She suspected money was going to be tight, but somehow he'd manage. He always had in the past.

As August dwindled to a close, Lanni could feel a new chill in the air. She gathered her sweater about her. Mentally she reviewed her confrontation with Charles. It had gone much worse than she'd expected. She'd been completely confident she was doing the right thing when she'd returned to Hard Luck.

Now she wasn't so sure.

When her brother had learned she had no intention of going home to Anchorage, he'd been outraged. He'd made his feelings on the subject extremely clear. He insisted she was throwing away an opportunity that might not come again.

It was true; she might not get another intern position at the newspaper. It was also true that if she didn't take this last chance to salvage their love, she'd regret it for the rest of her life.

But Charles didn't want her in Hard Luck, and now it looked as if her brother would find a way to send her packing.

Lanni hugged her legs and pressed her forehead against her knees.

Despite everything, Lanni couldn't forget the gleam in Ellen's eyes when she'd advised her to fight for Charles. What Ellen hadn't told her was how hard Charles would fight back.

Although she'd tried to hide it, his cruel words that afternoon had hit their mark. By remaining in Hard Luck, she was taking a risk—a risk that she might end up like her grandmother, loving a man she could never have.

She heaved a deep sigh, then lifted her head.

A shadow appeared, stretched across the still-bright ground. Lanni's heart quickened, not with fear, but with a breathless emotion.

It was Charles.

He didn't speak. She straightened her back, and her heart banged unmercifully against her ribs. For one wild moment Lanni wondered if her imagination had conjured him up. It didn't seem possible, after their confrontation earlier, that he was here.

Slowly she rose to her feet. She reached for the railing, needing the support. With a complete lack of haste, almost as if he was being drawn against his will, Charles approached her. One step at a time. One heartbeat at a time. One breath at a time.

When he was near, she could read for herself the wildness in his eyes. She could see his uncertainty, his pain. It hurt her to see him like this.

When she'd worked up the courage, she raised her hand and pressed it to his face.

Charles covered her hand with his and closed his eyes.

After a moment he opened them again. His gaze searched hers, and she felt the tension leave him.

"I'm tired of fighting a battle I can't win," he whispered. Then he pulled her, almost roughly, into his arms.

Lanni went willingly and buried her face in his neck. "It's about time!" she cried, wrapping her arms around him.

Not satisfied simply to hold her, Charles kissed her with an urgency that told her how difficult his struggle had been. The desperation she felt in him proved how very close she'd come to losing this battle.

Charles inched his mouth from hers with a reluctance that thrilled her. "I met with my mother this afternoon," he said, his voice low and ragged with emotion.

"Then you know about your uncle and . . . and the baby?" she asked gently.

Charles nodded. "Mother said she met with you earlier in the week."

Lanni nodded.

"She's happy, you know. Perhaps for the first time in her life."

They sat down on the porch steps. Charles on the top step, Lanni on the one below. He leaned down to clasp her hands with both of his.

"She told me how like my uncle Charles I am." He frowned as if even now he found it difficult to assimilate everything she'd said.

"It took a lot of courage for her to talk about him after all these years." Lanni hoped Charles could appreciate what it had cost his mother to share her secret.

"My father always loved Catherine."

"But he loved his brother more," Lanni whispered. "And he did love your mother."

"What you said about your being my destiny," he murmured, his hands cradling her face. "It makes sense now. It's as if everything is being made right through us."

"That's what I was trying to say earlier."

"I want us to get married, Lanni."

It took one millisecond for her head and her heart to grasp what he was saying.

"Married?"

"Don't tell me you've changed your mind."

"I haven't changed my mind." She laughed through her glistening tears. "Are you *nuts?*"

"I hope you don't want a long engagement."

"No. The shorter the better." Happiness filled her heart.

"I'm too old for you."

"Would you kindly stop making excuses?"

Charles grinned. His smile was lopsided and irresistible. Lanni moved to sit beside him and brought her mouth to his.

They kissed again and again as his restless hands roved her back. Finally he tore his mouth from hers, his breathing fast and heavy. His lips trailed the length of her neck, spreading kisses.

"Oh, Lanni, you tempt me."

"You do the same to me," she whispered.

He wrapped his arms about her. He didn't speak for several moments and seemed to be collecting his thoughts. "It sounds odd, but I think that my father has found a way to be with Catherine through me."

Lanni had similar thoughts herself. "It's almost as if he's . . . reached out from the other side and given us to each other."

"Yes, but I think he had a bit of help."

"His brother?" she asked.

"Yes, he's there with him." Charles kissed the top of her head. "I don't know what we're going to do about your internship," he said in a brisk, practical tone, as if he'd had enough of fate and fanciful notions and wanted to return to the reality of *their* lives.

"We'll figure out something later." A career in journalism didn't seem to matter all that much just then.

"But I thought journalism was important to you?"

Lanni pressed her back against him and settled into his arms. "It is, but I'd like to stay in Hard Luck. Perhaps publish a newspaper here."

"You'll need training and experience before you take that on. You'd have it, too, if you worked at the Anchorage paper."

"But, Charles, my commitment to it is for nine months. We'd have to delay the wedding. I don't think that's what either of us wants."

"I'm not going to change my mind about us marrying," he assured her. "I'm going to love you the rest of my life, Lanni Caldwell. I knew that the day Sawyer married Abbey. I know it now."

"I'd love to produce a newspaper for Hard Luck. But be warned, life might get a bit hectic, especially after we start a family."

"A family?"

"Children, Charles. You do want children, don't you?" She twisted around to look at him, her eyes suddenly worried.

He struggled for words, then nodded. "Yes, Lanni, I very much want children. With you."

"Oh, Charles." She shifted so that she faced him completely and took his face between her hands. "We're going to be so happy."

"Lanni—" he kissed her softly "—I think you're right."

* * * * *

Next month, join Charles, Lanni and your other
friends in Hard Luck—just in time
for Christmas! And find out what happens
when Mitch Harris meets Bethany Ross,
his daughter Chrissie's new teacher...
especially when Chrissie decides to become
Daddy's Little Helper *by trying*
to find him a wife!

If you enjoyed the Matchmakers by

DEBBIE MACOMBER

Here's your chance to order more stories by one of
Harlequin's beloved authors:

Harlequin Romance®

#03180	MY HERO	$2.79	☐
#03271	LONE STAR LOVIN'	$2.99	☐
#03307	READY FOR MARRIAGE	$2.99	☐

Harlequin® Promotional Titles

#83238	TO HAVE AND TO HOLD	$4.99	☐
	(short-story collection also featuring		
	Rita Clay Estrada, Sandra James, Barbara Bretton)		

By Request

#20100	MEN IN UNIFORM	$5.50	☐

(limited quantities available on certain titles)

TOTAL AMOUNT	$
POSTAGE & HANDLING	$
($1.00 for one book, 50¢ for each additional)	
APPLICABLE TAXES*	$_____
TOTAL PAYABLE	$_____
(check or money order—please do not send cash)	

To order, complete this form and send it, along with a check or money order
for the total above, payable to Harlequin Books, to: In the U.S.: 3010 Walden
Avenue, P.O. Box 9047, Buffalo, NY 14269-9047; In Canada: P.O. Box 613,
Fort Erie, Ontario, L2A 5X3.

Name:_____

Address:_____ City:_____

State/Prov.:_____ Zip/Postal Code:_____

*New York residents remit applicable sales taxes.
 Canadian residents remit applicable GST and provincial taxes.   HDMBACK3

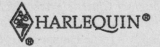

HARLEQUIN PRESENTS®

Harlequin brings you the best books, by the best authors!

LYNNE GRAHAM
Bestselling author of *Indecent Deception*

&

SANDRA MARTON

"Sandra Marton aims for her readers' hearts."
—*Romantic Times*

Coming next month:

***THE UNFAITHFUL WIFE* by Lynne Graham**
Harlequin Presents #1779

Leah wanted a divorce...but Nik didn't! Why *would*
Nik Andreakis want to hang on to the wife he'd been
blackmailed into marrying? And why—after ignoring
Leah for five long years—was Nik suddenly making
passionate advances toward her?

***HOSTAGE OF THE HAWK* by Sandra Marton**
Harlequin Presents #1780

Surely Joanna should despise Khalil? After all...the man
was holding her hostage! But Joanna had found heaven in
Khalil's embrace and now she wanted more...much more
from her "Hawk of the North"....

Harlequin Presents—the best has just gotten better!
Available in December, wherever Harlequin books are sold.